THE HALF-SISTERS

by *Cynthia Propper Seton*

THE HALF-SISTERS

THE SEA CHANGE OF ANGELA LEWES

THE MOTHER OF THE GRADUATE

A SPECIAL AND CURIOUS BLESSING

I THINK ROME IS BURNING

THE HALF-SISTERS

by

Cynthia Propper Seton

W · W · Norton & Company · Inc ·
New York

Library of Congress Cataloging in Publication Data

Seton, Cynthia Propper.
　The half–sisters.

　　I.　Title.
PZ4.S4957Hal　[PS3569.E8]　　　813'.5'4　　　　73–16155
ISBN 0–393–08689–5

Published simultaneously in Canada
by George J. McLeod Limited, Toronto

This book was designed by Margaret F. Plympton
The type is Caledonia and Janson.
The book was manufactured by the Vail-Ballou Press.

PRINTED IN THE UNITED STATES OF AMERICA
2 3 4 5 6 7 8 9 0

FOR *MAGGIE*

Contents

PART ONE 1937   7

PART TWO 1946   35

PART THREE 1970   105

PART ONE
1937

Chapter 1

On a hot Friday afternoon of midsummer 1937 Erica Thoroughgood, who was a hot plain child of eleven, sat still in her seat in the parlor car of the Cannonball, the express train to Montauk Point, waiting for it to get moving. She smiled shyly and wriggled a finger in goodbye to her mother, who was giving her another reassuring nod through the train window, and wished she would get moving. The car was filled with fathers who were off to join their families for the weekend on the second, better, end of Long Island, and one of these fathers in the seat next to Erica said to her, "Well, you are quite grown up to be traveling alone, my goodness!" and Erica said, "Oh, I have had to get used to it. I'm very nearly an orphan." The father swiveled into retreat. Immediately upon having told the whopper Erica was swept by a sickening fear of being found out, which was why eventually she gave up lying.

The truth was that under good President Franklin D. Roosevelt she was living through a very modern childhood marked by the number of children she knew with parents who divorced each other. The dread had set heavy in her heart that her own mother would divorce her father as the inevitable and most grand gesture of sophistication, so that when this was amicably accomplished the dread rolled off and out to sea.

When the train had crossed about an hour's worth of the flat sunny country the father in the next chair swiveled back to Erica, game for another encounter. "Where do you come from?" he asked her gently. Actually he looked like a *grand*father but not her grandfather, and, running her fingers from the twig with three red cherries appliquéd to the shoulder of her white linen dress down along the pleats to smooth them, she answered, "Oh well, I guess I don't come from anywhere." The grandfather pulled back again and she was sorry he heard her answers for rebuffs. She leaned toward him to be reassuring and continued, "My sister Billie comes from Center Moriches. She belongs there. You can tell. That's where I'm going. Only she's my half-sister." The grandfather no doubt looked in vain for things to pity in the round face with the sweet friendly grin. He saw short brown hair properly cut, good shoes, two plump knees rubbing each other for pleasure; a cared-for child. He could not say "What do you mean, 'nearly an orphan?'" and she could not explain who she was and where she had been born and the several places she had lived because even to her young ears she would have sounded the least abandoned of all children.

"Would you like to hear a coincidence?" she asked, intending to nail his attention in some other way. He would. "My sister Billie and I have two different mothers but we were born on exactly the same day, September 12. I was born at ten o'clock in the morning but she was born at night and so I am older." She did not say they had two different fathers, thinking it irrelevant. Being older than Billie was the only place Erica came out ahead. As it was the first serious thing they had established when they met, Billie had yielded a certain prior importance to Erica so that although Billie swam better, jumped higher, laughed louder, beat at checkers, and was called the tomato-eater, things were even-steven between them. Erica, who never won anything in the race against anybody but was always wistful that it might happen, Erica, who was not distinguished by any Moriches standards, certainly envied Billie and her yellow hair and her immense gift for disobedience but loved her with a full heart. She spent August, the month that fathers get the children, in Moriches with Billie and wished she belonged there.

Erica had no sense of physical place but she had a deep sense of belonging to her people. She was living now in a large apartment on Riverside Drive with her mother, who taught art history, and her grandmother, who was principal of P.S. 89, and her beloved grandfather, who was a lawyer, and a grown-up uncle and a cook and a maid, and not one of them could have stood it if she were kidnapped. Her concern about being kidnapped was not based upon probabilities. They weren't rich. They would have to get the ransom from Aunt Trudy, who was Billie's mother and her father's second wife. Aunt Trudy would surely give it, she hoped.

At the end of two hours along finally came Center Moriches. The white-coated porter handed her down to her father, and then her grip and the cartons of Schrafft's ice cream packed in dry ice. Billie was there skipping up in a ruffly pink sunsuit, freckled, peeling nose burned pink to match, and pale blue eyes smiling with mischief. No hello, just "Did you get vanilla?" after nearly one whole year. "Vanilla, chocolate, and coffee for Aunt Trudy." After supper they ran down to the end of the dock and threw the dry ice into the creek and watched the large milky-white bubbles pop-pop all over the place. If you touched dry ice it would burn you. Billie dared and it didn't. The tide was coming in and the *Exile II* bumped gently against the dock posts that were cushioned with pieces of rubber tire. A small cabin cruiser, it slept two and had a real stove you could cook at and a real toilet.

Erica's earliest Gothic romance with Moriches derived from a time before they were two separate families when her father had hired a boat for them to cross to the ocean beach to watch the total eclipse. It was terribly exciting not to see anything because of the clouds. Her father set her on his shoulders and told her the moon was going to cover the sun. "What if they bump?" she had asked. "Then the whole universe would burst in pieces." She waited for the first signs of that.

Aunt Trudy probably chose her father to be skipper more than to be husband and regretted it, Erica thought. Everybody said it suited him, the white yachting cap and jacket and leisure, because he was a writer and he needed not to be constantly brought up to the mark. "Here. You have him," Erica's busy mother must have said to Billie's, who had the time and the money. Their father had run the first boat aground and opened her hull and Aunt Trudy had to buy him another. Their father named the boats because he was a writer. The *Exile II* sounded a lot like the *Ittledo* but made less sense.

Erica's own mother was a slim little city woman and everybody obeyed her. Aunt Trudy was at least twice her size, an actress who had been pulled from the stage by heady passion, and was red and hearty with the grownups when she wasn't bitter white, and teased, scolded, and hugged children, but her bosom was so large as to be in the way of hugging back. She was always on the lookout for germs and kept Billie extremely healthy if skinny by cleaning her up ten times a day and cleaning her out with prune juice, nose drops, Castoria, green grapes, and celery, including the leaves. Billie almost always looked messy and outwitted her mother about the other regimen since she was often put on her honor, a thin reed. The children kept out of the way of Aunt Trudy, a matter of general preference, so that she could prepare the picnics.

There was no greater pleasure through Erica's sunny Moriches Augusts than the picnics on the boat. It was amazing how huge and dribbling the sandwiches were, leaking tomato and mayonnaise, and how everybody fit in the little square deck space, Aunt Trudy, their joint father, the two fat uncles, sometimes another guest or two, all wedged against the gunnels by an unfolded table covered with red and white checked oilcloth, everybody drinking beer and singing their heads off, "He shall die, he shall die, he shall die-de-i-die . . ." when they weren't quarreling in Dutch. Down the creek they headed and out across the bay to the sandbar, on the other side of which was the Atlantic Ocean. The two uncles came from Holland and had a store in New York where they sold diamonds and gave their money to Aunt Trudy, which was why she had a great deal. Erica and Billie sat legs straight on the varnished brown wood of the stern, the flag between them, and tried to break the varnish blisters with their fingernails while waiting till lunch. They were tough blisters. The water churned yellow with smoke below them and a little rowboat followed in tow with its nose in the air. There were three rainy days in August, the annual northeaster, and a few others, when they didn't go out on the boat.

"Don't you hope and pray it will be a nice day tomorrow," Erica asked Billie the first evening as they watched until the dry-ice bubbles would stop. From the end of the dock the sky took up most of the world. The creek was brimful and too wide to know who lived on the other side. Erica steeped her soul slowly into her summer life. She could smell the pleasure in the month ahead, she could taste it.

"I don't get much kick out of the boat any more. I just as

soon it rained," said callous Billie. It was the first sign for Erica of the spoilage of the future and the past.

The next morning was fine and hot and the one father lowered the two uncles and Aunt Trudy into the boat. Things were on course. Erica asked if she could put out the flag, if she could pull in the ropes, if she could start the engine, if she could steer. Billie, not herself, never entered that argument. Another was going between the uncles and Aunt Trudy in Dutch. Their father was at the wheel and spiritually well out of it, not knowing Dutch. "He eats the fruit in life and leaves me with the peelings," Aunt Trudy translated at the top of her lungs. "I know what he wants to do!" she bawled to the very "he." "He wants to get out! Drop me like he did the other. But he won't give up his toys, I bet you! There's not an ounce of manhood in him. He may fool others, ha!" She bared her teeth like a wolf and Erica was reminded of the experience Little Red Riding Hood had. Meanwhile, her father didn't seem to understand the English either.

So much did Erica hate the yelling that she spent the winter forgetting it. She scuttled to get out of earshot, and climbed to the roof of the cabin to be unembarrassed where Billie was silent on her belly. Erica believed Billie was suffering for shame that her parent was the bad parent, and tried to distract her by evoking their old dramatic fears about the creek mouth.

The creek spread out wide in flat country and was not a mile long. It came to one narrow conclusion in the middle of Main Street next door to the A&P grocery and at the other end contracted to a bottleneck built of black bulkheads, covered with barnacles, weeping with seaweed. Beyond was the bay. Aunt Trudy's house was halfway along, one of several setting like broody hens among their trees above the bibs of lawn burned to straw in the dry spell. Each lawn had a thin dock of wood planks in the shape of an L, one little bug leg kinked into the water, where there was either a small cruiser or a smaller motorboat tied or it was already out on the bay. Erica watched the land moving steadily by as if it were the shore that had the engine. They would be to the bay in a minute. In past summers the mouth of that creek regularly squeezed the breath out of her, frightened her silent. It was almost as narrow as a ferry slip and the *Exile II*, its engine slowing to a loud sputter, seemed to have to tuck in its sides to slither past the retaining walls, the water slapping loud and mad, before she was sprung free into the wide bay. But this summer while Billie lay flat, didn't lift her head, Erica, wailing oh-oh-oh in a low voice, failed even, little goose, to raise her own hackles. Above all the racket Aunt Trudy's voice asked, "How long am I expected to take it from him?" first in Dutch and then in English.

The old exciting fears that both children used to know how to raise in each other had a starboard side and a port. In the event that their father did not push straight out across the wide bay but went around the west bulkhead, which was only a sandy point, and followed the woodsy shore, they could come suddenly upon another creek, a secret creek, altogether the opposite from Aunt Trudy's wide open sunny one. Up it somewhere in the forest, they said, was an Indian settlement. One drizzly day when the children were little, their father said, "Let's have a look," and he nosed them along the dark thin little river overhung with heavy branches, where there were no children, no lawns, no boathouses, docks, mothers. "Do you hear drums?" Billie whispered, "I think I hear drums," and Erica had broken with terror and sobbed until they turned back.

The east bulkhead at the mouth of their own creek was the very opposite of wild. A fine flat deck of lawn, open as a fairway and carefully sprinkled green and cut trim, squared out to the sea wall. Well back behind heavy lilac bushes there was a large grey shingled house girdled by a wide apron of porch with white-painted pillars, and it was like a mother house watching with her arms crossed, and was in fact a mother house of a sort. Walk up their road to the end and you couldn't see in because of the thick hedge and the gate always closed, with a sign in iron saying Little Sisters of Charity, but from the boat you could sometimes spy nuns. There were mostly no nuns, or sometimes there were two nuns at a time, twin nuns. It was where they had their vacation, and it was a matter of interest to Erica that nuns would have a vacation. Moreover, they were white-habited instead of black, and they walked very slowly, moved nearly imperceptibly, the sea wind making them billow. The children were afraid of nuns.

Their fear was certainly compounded and ratified on a day when they saw a pair who did move, who were bending white and fluttery by the sea wall, looking down. "Do you think they've found a body?" Billie asked Erica. Billie enjoyed her fear but Erica did not. There was a second sinister thing about that green lawn coequal with the nuns on it. From time to time when somebody was drowned in the bay the undercurrents brought the body to the east bulkhead and it would be noticed bobbing limp against the wall where the crabs clung, people said.

In their relationship Erica was the suer and pursuer of her free-spirited, careless half-sister who used swear words. And this kept Erica awkward and uninteresting, the farthest cry from her true self. Sensing that everything familiar was turning untoward this first day of the new summer, she stopped saying oh-oh-oh and deferred mention of the nuns as there weren't any anyhow, and blurted out instead, "What's the matter with your hair?"

"I combed it with peroxide. You can get it at the drugstore if you say it's for your mother."

"You use peroxide?" Erica was unbelieving. In the race to be a grownup she was not even in the running in spite of being older, and jealously exploding she said, "I'm going to tell!"

"Oh what a goody-goody you are! Tell! See if I care." And with a lot of blond brass, Billie flopped over on her back and assumed the pose of a movie starlet who was way beyond listening to mothers. Erica was routed. She herself had the least possible awareness of the changes in her own body, not to say mind, consonant with being conscious, and none whatsoever in Billie's if you didn't count her hair.

The *Exile II* dropped anchor in the middle of the bay, from where you could not see the mouth of their creek landside and not see the dock at the ocean beach. They swam off the boat and then it was lunch and Aunt Trudy said, "Well Erica, how is the scholar? A-A on your report card, I bet you! My Billie doesn't use the brains she was born with. Billie! Look at Erica. Her mother doesn't have to tell her to do her homework I bet you!" The children looked at each other impassively, Erica suffering helplessly from goodness. The grownups had cold artichoke, crab salad, and white wine. Aunt Trudy had unpredictably become very hearty and kind to their father, who, however, did not encourage her to stay nice. He did not chat a little. The two uncles in their dark city suits grew fatter before your eyes, opened the top buttons of their trousers and took their naps. They were embarrassing.

Five or six other small boats were tied to the ocean dock when they reached it, and a large horseshoe crab lay in the shallows. Erica would never swim there, never. She threw saved picnic scraps out to the greedy squawking gulls. It was hot and still. The uncles woke up and began fishing from the stern of the tied boat. Their bait was a little pail of silver minnows flipping and flapping. It was too much to haul the two men out of the boat for the walk to the ocean, and besides they were mad about fishing.

On the long reef of sand that separated the bay from the

ocean nothing grew beyond sea grass, and there was no
place you could hide from the sun, no tree, no roof. The sand
was too scorching to walk on and the long narrow boardwalk
gave you splinters unless you wore sneakers. Aunt Trudy believed if you wore sneakers every day it ruined your eyes,
which seemed improbable. When Erica crested the low dune
and saw the ocean and got blown by the wind of it, when
she ran after Billie into the surf and flung her arms around
a swelling wave for love, she had won something in her
own way. Billie too. They became aquatic mammals, com-
manded and tamed the wild water, knew the way to take
the waves, which to let lift you up into the sky, which to
dive under, which to ride to the sand. The ocean equalized
them, and Erica loved Billie and was loved back. "You won't
tell my mother about my hair?" Billie asked. "I cross my
heart and hope to die," Erica assured her. All the way home
they were best friends.

Once Erica's father was back on land he cut a poorer figure. In the matter of the switch in households he had made,
she concurred with the general opinion that Aunt Trudy got
the worse end of the bargain. Aunt Trudy sometimes called
him foolhardy and sometimes spineless. Curiously, she didn't
know the rules against name-calling. One couldn't judge him
by ordinary standards because, being a writer, he didn't
have a job. Erica could not remember ever seeing him write,
or ever thinking that's what he was doing when he wasn't
around. From time to time she swayed with the surge of a
daughter's love and wanted to rescue his bad name, but he
wasn't friendly. Along with not being interested in work or
wives he was not interested in children. What he cared
about was the boat and a sports car with a rumbleseat he
drove as fast as summer lightning. Once in a very great
while he was willing to drive slower and let his daughters
ride in the rumbleseat. It was a tremendous treat but plainly
he didn't have fun.

Inside Aunt Trudy's house there was a large dark double parlor with her very good things and a polar bear rug having his mouth open. It was no place for children and, as grown-up life was lived on the porches in the summer, mostly empty except for Effie the colored maid, who was always cleaning it, and Aunt Trudy, who was showing her what she missed. Effie was the only one in the household who didn't look at Aunt Trudy when she was being talked to, not counting their father, and who walked right out in the middle of a paragraph when she had someplace else she wanted to go. Erica loved Effie best and Effie loved Billie best, a natural situation to which Erica had long been resigned.

The dinner table was round with a lazy susan in the middle and the nightly row was circular, and whatever one person said cut no ice with the next. Aunt Trudy had taken a position which was that if their father couldn't write because of the muse, then he should get a job at the diamond store. Uncle Derick said, "Over my dead body." Uncle Anton said, "Sales are down again. We aren't hiring." Aunt Trudy said, "Business is very good." Their father said, "The beef is tough." So the argument went round and round through the summers, nothing changing because the men were always in agreement it shouldn't. Their father wasn't going to take the job in the diamond store and the uncles weren't going to let him have it. They evidently liked disobeying Aunt Trudy, or at least they never seemed to tire of it. "By God," Uncle Derick would say, "my fingers are itching to cast for blues," and then everybody knew that within the next few days the men would go deep-sea fishing by themselves, and that their father would take them in the boat across the bay and through the inlet and out into the ocean for bluefish and weakfish in spite of Aunt Trudy's scoldings. "That cruiser's too light for the ocean!" "One day you'll see!" "What a foolhardy thing to do!" For three or

four days they'd play her at the end of the line, a practice
fish, and then one morning before dawn off they would have
gone.

For the most part the quarreling grownups were out at
the periphery, and indeed defined the periphery, of Erica's
summer world. They were like sentinels, and wide-awake, as
you could hear by the shouting, and while Aunt Trudy quite
fiercely enforced some regimental rules about bedtime and
wearing sneakers she was otherwise amazingly unobservant
and Billie got away with a million things. The freedom was
blissful for Erica. All winter she was superintended, admired, loved, instructed, improved. August was a breather.
It was a safe private child's month in which she and Billie
passed the long days by themselves making believe. Not
this summer. A couple of nights on they were in their beds
and Erica rolled out with innocent confidence their ritual
"I hate boys, don't you?" and Billie announced, not only in
betrayal of their being just two best friends together, but
with indifference to the betrayal, "I'm crazy about them."
Billie had let the outsiders in. "I know a lot of boys," she
said in her impish way, "and I'll show you them if you promise not to tell."

The next afternoon in the solitary time before supper she
whispered, "Come on!" and led the way behind the barn,
which was made into a garage, and past the huge yellow
sunflowers that grew like soldiers in a row as high as the
roof against the old empty chicken house; but it was now
the secret clubhouse with four long skinny boys who looked
all alike, and a girl, Eunice. "That's Erica, my sister from
the city that I told you about," Billie said in a nice way, because Billie was a good sport, which everybody always remarked. "This is the gang," she said to Erica. So from then
on Erica was the outsider and practically every day after
they'd come in from the boat they played spin-the-bottle in

the middle of the chickenhouse floor with Eunice and the faded blond skinny boys who all wanted to kiss Billie and absolutely did not want to kiss Erica.

It was one dreadful rite of passage for Erica and introduced her to every sort of shame without bringing any compensating benefits. She stood stiff, nearly numb, with her knees pressed together at her place in the circle while the empty milk bottle was spun, and didn't at all want to be kissed, but did want to be somebody. They needed a lookout and would she be the lookout and they liked her for one minute after she said all right, and then they forgot her. All the good things she was had no currency here. All the bad things they plainly thought—her being a tag-along baby and a bad sport and a coward—she could not gainsay. After that first time Billie never even wanted her to come. For several days she was lookout but after the boat was in nobody ever came that way, and once she had to go to the bathroom very badly. She wondered over the astonishing discrepancy between now and her city life, where she was the world's most important child.

So she stood dumb and foolish curled round the chicken house door with the squeals and giggling at her back. Inside there was hardly any daylight, and there were cobwebs, spiders, bugs, flies, and dismaying dirt everywhere. Wisps of straw blew across the rotting floor, and one way she was a coward was that she was afraid to be inside and not only because of bats, which she never raised her eyes to search the rafters for. The other way was to be so reduced by envy that she couldn't make herself not come each time. Little nothing, little slave shriveled body and soul against the doorpost, Erica looked out across a yellow field with the sun coming down to make her squint, and never heard anybody and never saw anything, not even the creek, which was hidden by the high grass.

Then one afternoon the boat was still out because of the deep-sea fishing expedition and Erica drew a little flutter of attention by being on the lookout with something to look out for. "She's got a very important job," Billie said to the generality, and the club members stared at Erica in a serious way. "You have to listen with all your might," Billie warned her in a kind of pep talk. So Erica stood at her post and listened and almost immediately the sound of a boat engine approached and slowed and choked to a stop and Erica bolted inside to warn them, "Here they are! They're back!" and everybody scattered to the darkest corner and lay low and Erica was included completely. Very soon there was the sound of feet coming up the path and Erica thought how nimble the fat uncles could be if they had a mind, and they heard men's deep voices. And they weren't the voices of Aunt Trudy's men.

To have another boat at their dock was an unprecedented event and in a split second the crouching Erica and the crouching Billie united in a glance, re-allied by curiosity. The club meeting was over for that day. At the All Clear the other members skitted off the property through the rhododendron bushes, and when they were well gone, Billie and Erica emerged from the henhouse and, swinging their arms with an air of the greatest innocence, strolled across the meadow grass to see what boat.

"My golly, it's a Coast Guard boat!" Billie said with reverence and joy.

"My golly, it's the Coast Guard!" Erica echoed. There was a large cruiser, much larger than the *Exile II,* and spanking white, much whiter; the Coast Guard had the whitest boats of all. The best. You could see them a million miles away. United States Coast Guard was printed grandly in neat black letters at her bow and on the life preservers, and the flag!

"I've never in my whole life seen one this close, I swear to God," Billie said. "I once heard they were not allowed to have one spot on her. After they rescue somebody they have to bring her in and paint her fresh. It's the law."

"It's the law."

After a few minutes of examining her for spots and finding plenty, they began to wonder why she was at their dock and raced up to the house, Billie beating. Effie was just coming after them, she said. They said she would never guess in a million years what was down at the dock and she said a Coast Guard boat. It was only then that it occurred to Erica there was probably a bad reason for this. Here she beat Billie, who would have bounced off to tell her mother but was caught in Effie's grip and told to pay attention. Effie passed out sticks of chewing gum and said they weren't to disturb the two Coast Guardsmen in their uniforms who were in the double parlor explaining to Aunt Trudy.

"It's the *Exile II*! She must have had an accident!" It now dawned upon Erica.

"Everybody's going to be all right," Effie said, "but it broke in half at the inlet. It was very rough out there this afternoon."

"Broke in half?" Billie gasped.

"Split right in two, your mother say."

"What about our father?" Erica asked. "And the uncles?" she included politely.

"They up in the hospital at Riverhead but they say they going to be jes fine. They have exhaustion. And you not to worry now whilst your mother's going to visit up there in a police car, and you going to stay right here with me and we going to have spaghetti."

"Police car!" said Billie, who jumped and wriggled some more and could not believe the string of good luck. "Come on, Erica, let's see if it's in the driveway." Holding hands tight with Effie, they went to see the police car in the driveway. It was Billie's speed. All this was Billie's speed. Tell her not to worry and she didn't worry. Erica slipped her arm around Effie and began to cry. "What a crybaby you are, Erica. Nobody's hurt, they said. They're just exhausted." That was Billie.

They had their spaghetti at the kitchen table with Effie, and a long time later Aunt Trudy never even came in to kiss them goodbye when she went in the police car. Finally they could watch from the window if they were quiet when the two Coast Guardsmen in their white uniforms walked back down toward the dock. Silly Billie skipped around and talked her head off and wouldn't obey Effie. The next morning Aunt Trudy was still visiting the hospital and it was like a holiday. A lot of people came to talk to Effie, and Billie was peeking around the house at them and wriggling and mimicking and finally Erica snapped, "Shut up! You're the baby! Don't you see something very bad's the matter?" And it was a miracle. Billie all at once restored to Erica her seniority and authority.

Just before lunch while they were straggling about outside not doing anything, a grey limousine driven by a chauffeur came into their driveway to strike them with more awe, and when it stopped out of it came the most unexpected person of all, Erica's own dear New York grandfather to whom she belonged. She ran into his arms and cried, "Something terrible has happened and nobody has told us what it is." "I'll tell you," he said in his quiet dear familiar voice, and she knew she would survive the news.

Whenever Erica's grandfather was in charge, civilization worked, and worked civilly. People turned over their troubles to him and got calm. She was immensely proud that he loved her best of anybody in the world. However, this left her fencing with a fear that he would die soon because he was so far ahead, being a grandfather. He was a handsome man with deep brown fine wise eyes and he said they would talk in the car on their way back to the city. How tremendous to buy a car just to pick her up, and a chauffeur since he didn't drive. No, he said, he had rented them at the garage on 85th Street. Tremendous enough to know they had an extra. Finally settling in her best white city dress against the grey upholstery of a limousine, this other bad business still at bay, she was nearly dizzy with the sense of her own importance. Hovering at the edge of her mind was the knowledge that she would hear her father had drowned, but she hadn't heard it yet. She did not know how to look while listening to news of such dramatic dimension. And here it came.

"I'm going to tell you a story of true heroism, Erica," her grandfather said, taking her hand, speaking thoughtfully the way he did. "And your father was the fine hero of it." This was praise indeed from her grandfather, who did not stand for any nonsense.

"You know," he said, "I've often thought that if your father had been born in an earlier time he would have run away to sea when he was a boy. He had such a taste for derring-do, for adventure." He crinkled his eyes as if to clear a film from them so that he could think more clearly and then went on. "As to what happened yesterday, it seems that they had had a fine day fishing, and that he was bringing the boat back toward the inlet where the water is always turbulent. The Coast Guard tell us that by noon the waves were six feet high. All white water. They were cruising the area, on the alert. Two other boats had hailed them already and they'd taken one of them in tow. Well, it was about two-thirty and a particularly high tide when they saw the *Exile II* in trouble. She seemed to be out of control, tossed this way and that by those powerful waves. So they turned about and headed right to her but before they reached her, in front of their very eyes she was flipped over by a heavy wave and cracked in half. They went full speed, as fast as they could manage, watching while the two halves of the boat divided and were being carried off in different directions . . ."

"And my father was drowned," pronounced the dry-eyed

child in a rush, this knee-rubber, this great book reader who always needed to look at the end first.

"Your father, you know, was a powerful swimmer and he was trying to reach Uncle Anton. Uncle Anton was struggling terribly in the choppy water and couldn't swim at all. The Coast Guard boat came as close as possible. They had to be careful not to run them down, you see. And they threw life preservers to them and your father grabbed the nearest one and with powerful determination he shoved it to Uncle Anton and saved his life. That showed his true mettle, you know. How many of us in a moment of crisis would prove to be selfless? Very few, probably. Very few."

"You would," said Erica, knowing she wouldn't. She wasn't even crying. "And then what happened, Grandpa?"

"Ah well, that's the sad thing. Then the Coast Guard can't fathom what did happen. At one moment there was your strong father. And then they couldn't find him anywhere. With their boat hook they hauled in the nearest half of the *Exile II* and under it they found Uncle Derick half conscious in the air pocket. He had managed to wedge himself into the overturned bench. That saved him." And so finally she did cry in her grandfather's arms and when she was all finished she said, "Well, I guess my father showed Aunt Trudy!"

Later they stopped at a lovely outdoor restaurant and had their lunch under a red and white striped umbrella. Erica saw with relief that she was too distracted to eat very much, because she also saw that she had no very sad sense of loss. She hid this carefully. For days and weeks she lived in fear they would tell her that her father's body had drifted to the sea wall and the nuns had found it. She badly didn't want to hear it.

Chapter 2

Once back in the fortress of her apartment house, her own high strong solid home full of reading lamps and sofa pillows, and good old New Jersey out the window and good old Grant's Tomb, Erica stitched her mind closed against Moriches into a magic sack of safety, obsessively, like an old gnarled crone in an old gnarled wood. It was a charm against further drownings of family members, and against any more mortifications in chicken houses. In the event, the charm worked excellently well in the matter of domestic fatalities, but did not ward off that root mortification. Nobody bound her to Billie any more, a loss she did grieve for, all the while knowing that old breezy Billie would mind for one second not to be sisters and forget the next second. And what were they going to do out there without a boat, and without a skipper?

Very pleasantly, it seemed to Erica, she was singled out by the drift of wills to be the only one left to bear the name of Thoroughgood. There were some Thoroughgood cousins of her father who lived near Norfolk, Virginia, but he had long ago seceded absolutely from the South. Of the two women he had married, the first, Erica's mother, was always called Ellen Phillips to make it clear as possible that although she was not a man she was a serious scholar committed to American art history and everybody in the field had better reckon with her. And to prove it she went about hunting up limners' portraits in Vermont and buying them for a song right under their noses. In Erica's room there was an old woman painted on wood boards with a white ruffled cap, probably thinking she was smiling but actually looking mad as the devil. Erica was taught to call her mother Ellen as a sign of how modern Ellen was.

It was thought that Ellen Phillips regarded her daughter, albeit with love and pride, as the issue of a dalliance. She did not belabor herself with this early romantic error, and was not distressed by the weak choice, it seemed. The error was made in Paris in the year *Ulysses* was carried about and Hemingway was moving restless through its streets, and Tom the poet and Ellen the pregnant art student had not known of the existence of either the literary event or the literary man. Later Tom went around saying that he certainly did. In the end, tidy, ambitious, *truthful* Ellen bit him off firmly as a thread, as if she had finished sewing that seam. She wasn't ungrateful to him. After all, she wouldn't have had Erica without him.

Tom seemed to have been put down as a dalliance by Billie's mother too.

On a wintry school night when they were all at dinner, Erica's grandfather asked Erica's mother, "Who do you think called me at the office today, Ellen?"

"I can't imagine, Papa."

"Well, my dear, it was old Tom's Trudy."

"Come out of her cuckoo house? What could she possibly want with you?"

"She said that she had a few legal matters to discuss of an extremely personal nature, and that there was no other lawyer she could think of in whom she could more safely trust her . . ."

"Oh, that woman is absolutely tasteless," said the elegant tiny Ellen in a mild voice with her long throat stretched as a mark of the best taste. "Poor sweet Papa," she continued affectionately, "the way you are adored by hysterical women . . ."

"Impoverished hysterical women," he qualified.

Meanwhile, sweet papa's wife, Erica's grandmother, who was the principal of P.S. 89 and a great knitter of afghans, looked impatiently at her husband and said, "Oh what a floozy that woman is! What was she after? Besides you?"

"She's unstable, Mother, but she's not a floozy," said Ellen.

"There were a few things," said her grandfather, after one strong clarifying blink of his eyes. "She wants to resume the use of her former name, Van Brink." Terrific thought Erica. That was Billie's name, Wilhemina Marie Van Brink, and it was an entirely good idea for Aunt Trudy to match.

And so it transpired that Erica was the only Thoroughgood, and was left to grapple with the ironic pleasure of a name like that. It was also how her connection with Billie was never broken although Aunt Trudy was an endless bother to her grandfather. However, Erica grew up never going to Moriches again, never seeing Billie once, although she heard this and that. Billie went off to boarding school in Bridgeport, Connecticut, by the Port Jefferson ferry. Uncle Derick died in bed of natural causes.

Erica herself lived through a tremendous uneventful normality, looking like the most average caterpillar waiting interminably to break out and be dazzling. She evened off at middle height, with brown hair and brown eyes, a middle color. Her girlhood was entirely a condition of preparation and every year of it was in the shade, in the anteroom, in the dentist's chair, learning, practicing, getting straightened out. Or, to put it differently, she chugged down this stretch of track with stolid resignation like the good little engine since that was the only way you arrived, you got to the last stop, twenty-one, faultless, beyond criticism. Her impatience to get to the end alternated with her relief that she hadn't, that there was still time for a miracle of transmogrification in which the intelligent wholesome Erica could become sultry and stunning and popular with the boys. To this end she would not necessarily have sold her birthright nor traded her stout-minded family in for one that was less sure about wrong steps and bad habits.

The true ruler of her family attempted to be her grandmother, who had a certainty about matters large and small that was marvelously tenacious. She spent all day long being principal in her junior high discerning and correcting the poor judgment and poor taste of the entire student body, the only sort of judgment and taste they seemed to have, and at four on the button came through the door to be principal at home and correct Erica for saying "Hi!" for saying "Sure!" and to warn her against her tendency to be common. Under her grandmother's suzerainty Erica was the subject with the fewest rights but the most love. The list of things she was not allowed to do that everybody else was allowed to do, beginning with not wearing lipstick and silk stockings and high heels, became the longest in New York City.

Her grandmother ruled by imperturbability and did not raise her voice. She gave looks. Everybody got his own looks. The ones to her grandfather put him down for being so easily flattered by a pretty face and for clutter because he couldn't expect Bridie, who was the maid, to do a thing about the books piled on the floor and papers that should be thrown out. When her grandmother set her upper row of teeth inside her lower it was a sign that her grandfather had taken one or the other of these bad steps. Putting her jaw this way made her look more pensive than angry but actually she was angry. Toward her daughter Ellen, Erica's mother, she was extremely patient for her not marrying again and having her own home. Ellen *nearly* would marry, and then she didn't, at least twice. When she teetered about Mr. Caplan, whom Erica had found not only terrific but handy, since he worked at the Metropolitan Museum and he could just take the 86th Street crosstown bus, her grandmother said to her mother one day, "Do what you like, Ellen. It's your choice, of course. One is concerned that an unmarried woman is condemned to a partial life. Marriage is normal to the species."

"Well, Mother, it wouldn't be fair to marry where I don't really love."

"That seems naïve to me, Ellen. Hollywood invented that kind of love, a cheap veneer of glamour over the animal business, a romantic convention. It doesn't exist."

"If she doesn't love him, Erica, then she would be wrong to say yes," said her grandfather reliably in direct contradiction, on one of their private Sunday-morning walks through the park. "Each of us has to resist a great deal of pressure to do what everybody else thinks he should do. Sometimes they're right, of course."

There was for Erica a steadying quality in her family under the management of her grandmother. Everyone firmly did not take her advice and as the years passed they were like buoys and landmarks, remaining steadily who they were. Wilson was a *light*house. Everybody tried to find a solution to him, but he was moody and racked up demerits in school and out and not only didn't he get into Harvard, but didn't stay in City College. Woodrow Wilson Phillips was her mother's brother and nineteen the summer of the drowning, much too old to be friends but unusually young for an uncle. Basically, he did not find anything to interest him notwithstanding the number of suggestions and examples brought to his attention.

It was against Wilson that Erica took a twofold measure of herself. First, she was excellent in every worthy thing and he wouldn't even try, and thereby was a small constant against which she stood nine feet tall. To love books, to get A's, to be friendly, to have a good French accent, were congruous to her nature, which was her luck. He had the reverse luck. And second about Wilson, she could never attract his interest. He blotted her out. He would bump into her at the elevator and not even say hello, borrow her dollars and not be thankful. Even if she had some terrific thing to tell him that he really wanted to know, he'd grab that thing and hug it to him like a football and duck off with it in a second, not giving her credit at all. Yet Erica could not recall a time when she was unaware that this odd sulking uncle was ballast to her overblown self-importance. That is to say, Wilson may have been serving himself poorly but he was of some negative use to her, a daily reminder until he went to the war that there was extant in the world a vantage point from which she, Erica Thoroughgood, could be seen to be of no consequence whatever. Almost consciously she registered this corrective.

The war was certainly not the way Erica's grandmother planned to solve Wilson. Quite the contrary. Her grandmother was firmly and finally against war *tout court,* and the Spanish Civil War made her furious. At two different luncheons she had shaken hands with Mrs. Roosevelt about peace but Mrs. Roosevelt was giving in. War was coming anyway, said her grandfather, and it became a critical household matter. With her grandmother bullheadedly stranded higher and dryer, Erica felt constrained to approach her own mother: "What are we ever going to do about Grandma and the war, Ellen?" "Well, we won't make her fight," said Ellen, who had long followed a policy of appeasement.

Erica tracked down her grandfather in his white shirt in his dark room with his books and his papers and his bed. "It will break Grandma's heart," she said. "She has such high principles!"

"Well, after all, Erica, what are we to do?" said her grandfather, who rested his orange Parker fountain pen and his yellow writing pad on his long crossed leg. "Here is Germany now, overcome with an insane viciousness. She is spilling over her borders to conquer other countries, murdering . . . hating. She will not stop. Unbelievably, this once civilized country is hounding her own Jewish people who are innocent, who are industrious, loyal . . . pulling them out of their houses, thousands upon thousands of them, herding them into ugly prison camps, with their little children crying and bewildered . . . as if the Jews were terrible criminals when they are only ordinary citizens living the kind of ordinary lives we live. What is Roosevelt to do?"

What was Roosevelt to do? There were moments when she forgot which was President Roosevelt and which was her grandfather. She fused their wisdom, their noble handsome heads, so that when her grandfather frightened her sometimes by a kind of lofty uninvolvement, there was FDR in his black cloak and his rumpled felt hat leaning out of his touring car, out of the newsreel on Saturday afternoons with a smile of tremendous patriotic American love and reassurance. Her grandmother must surely succumb in the movies.

"Is a strike a good thing or a bad thing?" Erica remembered asking her grandfather when she was little. "It is both," he said, archetypically detached, not showing her the right side to be on, detaching her.

"Grandpa," she said later when she was older, "I really think Wilson isn't happy."

"Nobody says you have to be happy," said her grandfather.

Sometimes with his not believing in the inevitability of progress, in that necessary march toward a better world that America was leading, she was brought to take a look over the chasm and see for an awful instant what it might mean really to be free of all illusions. It was President Roosevelt who pulled her back. Central to her pride in her intellectual atheist liberal New Deal family was the certainty that they were way out ahead, dealing with reality. That they were on the right side of history, the right side of the Atlantic, not that they had exchanged one set of illusions for a more modern one.

Finally war came and was a relief. They'd been watching a football game at the Polo Grounds on a freezing dark afternoon and the loud speaker interrupted the game to page two generals. When they got home it had been Pearl Harbor. Immediately her grandfather settled bent by the radio and began to monitor the course of the war. Erica was immensely excited, and mobilized the several intentions she had to live a dedicated life—although dedicated to what? Entirely unexpectedly, so must Wilson have done that. He announced the next night at dinner, "Well, I joined the Merchant Marine today." Erica's grandmother was allowed to slip in on the side of the Allies, everybody pretending from then on that her patriotic record wasn't poor. She stopped knitting afghans and started on sea boots, enormous long thick white stockings that came up to the thigh. Erica was fifteen.

PART TWO

1946

Chapter 3

Erica became twenty somehow, no thanks to Ellen, who had turned unstable for what everybody allowed tacitly to be a moderately good reason. Mr. Caplan had married somebody else. He had been on her string for some years where she kept people. Why his disaffection should have rocked Ellen was thought to have more to do with her passing a lonely forty, still handsome, elegant, and a size 8, but stalled for some time in her progress toward the top of her field. She was superior as ever but not gentle, not suffering fools gladly, and by and by they stopped suffering her. There was a lack of authority and title in her present situation and this inspired a twisted need in her, evidently, to recast the story of her life, letting Erica have glimpses of a carefree but luscious naughtiness that she now recalled characterized her younger years. She had been the center of so many romantic adventures as finally, for want of time, to have impeded her professionally. It wasn't a matter of just one roll in the French hay, no, no. Erica winced.

"Of course when I was your age, Erica, I had been living abroad for some time—in a fairly cosmopolitan set, actually. As a matter of fact, one of the daughters of the Duke of Devon . . ." Erica closed her ears to it, hummed to shut it out, and said to herself, "The Duke of Devon! The Duke of Devon! I'm going to be sick . . ."

Ellen, her usual self a truth-bearer, would proceed through time in the conventional way and then suddenly stop and roll backward down her nether side, lying. It was as though her sexual excitement were retrospective. Erica's grandfather said that in regard to sex the family position was a somewhat hysterical denial.

Erica had grown to be a handsome girl with a self-confidence based upon intellectual and esthetic achievement, but subverted by at least fifty double features a year, not to mention the probably unconscious effects of the family sexual policy. She had the kind of promising beauty that satisfies the vanity of mothers and grandparents, sensible and in good taste. She would have given her eyeteeth to be cute. The stirring of her own sensuality caused her shame. The war had allowed her some peace in growing up by putting all the boys in the Army. When they finally came home they sorted themselves out, the ones calling her up being the ones she couldn't bear to be with.

"For goodness sake, Erica," her grandmother said twenty times, "how you fend off these nice young men! Just go out and have a good time. You don't have to marry them!" This was unhelpful advice, this having a good time. She shriveled like the Wicked Witch of the North to be touched by most boys, and touch her most boys would. There were a hundred miserable gambits in the dating ritual, ninety-nine of them a way of touching.

Alex Miller was a boy with whom she had a fairly earnest romance by correspondence for the three years he was overseas, but when he was back in the States he took the train up to Smith to see her, clearly with great reluctance. Erica, anticipating this approach of what was after all a total stranger thinking he had a claim of some sort upon her, was all set to shrink from him when there he was, enduring the visit, enduring her, saying it took a lot of time to get one's bearings after a war like that. Simply to be a friend to a boy was what she didn't know how to do at all. Neither did she have the language, nor the models. To walk along the edge of the Pond in the hazy orange autumn not even holding hands was harder than being knocked down and pawed at and breathed over. But Alex didn't want her. Chilled, she drew up her cover, explained how important she was, how sophisticated, sometimes in French, discussed the House Committee on Un-American Activities, her belief in trial marriages, meaning of course in time and without suggesting for a split second that she would try one with Alex, and said she was thinking of applying to law school but would-she, wouldn't-she go? That this boy needed cover, a comforter, never occurred to her until after his train had gone. He had really been in a real war, had crossed to Normandy on D-Day, seen awful suffering and live bodies die, got frostbite himself in the Battle of the Bulge and lost two toes, not glorious, but his toes. Back in America he found everybody unbearably jarring. Erica, superior as she proved she was, knowing so much, didn't begin to imagine what his reality was made of. He left town with barely decent haste, left her blushing, blushing on the station platform.

"Have you and Alex broken apart, dear?" Ellen asked her at Christmas. "Broken apart! Broken apart! Ugh! Disgusting!" she hummed to herself, and aloud said, one liar to another, "Goodness, Ellen, we were never together in the first place. I'm seeing somebody else entirely, a guy who's a senior at Amherst and who . . ."

"After all, I know something of what you must be going through . . ." and off Ellen went, klippity-klop, preposterous, at the very moment her daughter had got interested in cooking up a story of her own. Fatefully, as it turned out, Erica was invited to expand upon her story by her grandmother, principal emeritus who had become very old with arthritis and had difficulty getting around but not difficulty hearing what one private person thought she was saying privately to another.

"Erica, do I understand there is a new young man in whom you have some interest?" she asked, expressing herself with her usual precision, wanting a precise answer, very keen to have Erica launched, and no wonder, with the bad marriage record of her own two children.

"Yes and no, Grandma, yes and no," Erica said with a sigh and a laugh. Only two days into vacation and already every one of them had proved unbearable. They were all sitting over dinner coffee, and from her chair she saw through the arch to the hallway the lamplight shine on the hard floor, and beyond to the living room more lamplight soften the browns and beiges, show how beautiful the Christmas tree was and the great worn Bokhara rug. They were all looking at her, she knew, even tamed Wilson and his dopey wife Muffie (Muffie! Can you beat it? From California!). After all, where else would they have to look?

"Are we going to meet him, dear? I'm sure we would all like to meet him. We would be very discreet," said her grandmother, believing she spoke with a delicate wit.

"To be discreet," Ellen said, "is the second precaution in a love affair. I hope I don't have to tell you, Erica, the first. The first . . ."

"You're talking nonsense, Ellen," said Erica's grandfather.

"You might at least tell us his name, dear. We won't breathe a word to the *Times*," her grandmother pursued. She was getting dotty . . . from the pain-killers maybe.

"His name is Frank Ryan and he was in the Navy and he's

a senior at Amherst and he wants to go to law school." Absolutely all she knew about him right there!

"Just like you!" squealed dopey Muffie.

"More, he wants to go much more than I do," said Erica. She knew that too about him. What a grind . . . no, not a grind but how . . . ruthless he was—or self-centered. He wants what he wants, that guy. Boy, he's so sure of himself. God.

"He must be Catholic with a name like Ryan," said Wilson. Where there was a wrong thing to say out loud Wilson could be counted on. And Frank, as a matter of fact . . . his religion . . . what a hypocrite. Not a hypocrite exactly but . . .

"I knew I had something to tell you, Ric," said her grandfather, first blinking out Wilson. "Who do you think it was called me today but your old Aunt Trudy? And she had some news for you. She says Billie is engaged to be married. What do you think of that?"

"Married! Why she's only my age, twenty . . . she couldn't have finished . . . married! No kidding! Who to?"

"To *whom,* my dear, to *whom.* Twelve hundred and fifty dollars for room and tuition, you know, ought to secure you in the English language," said the witty grandmother.

"Now let's see," said her grandfather, reaching into his breast pocket for his index card of reminding notes. "His name is something-something Ives. He is a bona fide Westhampton Beach Ives sure enough. I believe I am right when I say that I am entrusted to convey in properly solemn tone the magnificence of this catch. No date has been set for the wedding but Billie has said—as I understand her mother—Billie has said that she would not consider marrying without her dear sister Erica there to wish her well."

"The Iveses! Goodness, her mother will love that," said Ellen.

Her family were all loving it and Erica was simulating her love of it. She sensed that they liked the goad it poked into her, a little tit for tat in payment for the touch of condescension in her manner when she returned home for her vacations. They talked very knowingly about Moriches and Billie, what a little harebrain she was as a child but how spunky. That she would get an Ives with a mother like that was simply a miracle. When their flurry of interest in the subject subsided they forgot all about it.

But Erica trailed through the next days, through present buying, through double-dating, through an egg nog party, *Swan Lake* at the City Center and Christmas Eve at home, looking as languorous as possible in her mother's tight short beaver jacket through which all the wet river wind blew to the bone easily, with a long full black skirt of nun's veiling that caught in her spiked heel and in the doors of buses, subways, and elevators. She did not break her neck or get pneumonia. She looked at herself in every possible reflecting glass for promise, and always an inconclusive self looked back.

It wasn't Billie's social coup but the untimeliness of her move that cut Erica down. It was like poor sportsmanship . . . to dart ahead that way. It was like not taking turns, not being fair, for after all there was a muted understanding among her sort, wasn't there, that they were meant to play out their lives on a heroic scale but that they had not yet entered the proscenium where the heroes waited. College was anticipatory, four years blocked out under the agreement. You might play the field, you might be crazy about a boy, but marriage! Not marriage. Billie's romantic fact trumped Erica's romantic fancy. Real life was right now. That was Billie's news. The real scene right here and the extraordinary men this very moment were not waiting, but were getting fascinated and falling in love with girls who pushed ahead.

"Oh, is that so!" she said, and that's why she got all dressed up. Nothing happened, but through Christmas her spirits rose anyway. And her grandmother or mother would tweak her about the Amherst romance and, tasting ginger, she would tweak them back with imaginative touches of silence or "It's really nothing!" or "I honestly don't want to talk about it!" Then the craziest thing happened. On the afternoon of New Year's Eve she had no more than come through the door when her mother pounced and in a loud important whisper, just grotesque, said "Erica. Your friend has called. Mr. Ryan. I have the number right here. Topping something. Isn't that a Bronx exchange?"

"Mmn," said Erica as if she were not startled. "I'll take it in the bedroom." Her grandmother, who had propped herself in the doorway for a better view, said, "I think it might be Riverdale." Oh great equalitarians, those two women.

Ryan's voice: "Hi, baby! Listen, Thoroughgood, I'm in a kind of a jam and I was hoping you might be able to help me."

"I thought you lived in Boston."

"I do live in Boston, but at the last minute I got this ride down with my brother and a buddy of his on condition once we got here I'd make myself scarce. . . . They have these dates for New Year's Eve. . . . Well, the fact of the matter is I've called every Y in the city and they're all filled. . . . I'd probably run into the same luck at the Waldorf-Astoria . . ." He waited, offering her the opportunity to say something, which she did not take. She had once read in a magazine that whoever began a sentence with "The fact of the matter is" was lying.

"I wonder," he continued in a firm voice with a trace of impatience, "if you might happen to have an extra bed?" She was silent, in the exact middle between yes and no.

"You think I've got a lot of crust, don't you?"

"Yes," she said "but come over anyway."

"Listen, I really appreciate this. I think you're great."

Well, the two ladies of the house were very knowing and both went into Wilson's room to see that it was in order. Bessie the cook stood in the doorway, annoyed about the fuss. Little squat Bridie stood behind her all set in her coat, hat, galoshes, umbrella, pocketbook, brown paper bags, to go off to her family in Yonkers for the holiday. Erica, back in the black skirt, the white shirtwaist, the ponytail with the black ribbon, held her hands behind her, rolled her eyes at the sight of them all, and said "God" and said "Honestly" and thought she looked quite in the spirit of Degas's bronze ballerina with the rotting tutu. The doorbell rang and her grandmother, her mother, Bessie, and Bridie turned round in a row. No help for it. No help for any of what would follow, and Erica greeted long thin Ryan, who was buttoned into a Navy pea jacket, and thought, "Sure. That's what he looks like," and introduced him to the four women and he shook hands with all four of them and said, "Pleased to meet you." Honestly.

She led him confidently into Wilson's room with the north window framing the bridge, the span strung now with lights. On Wilson's bed was spread the handsomest afghan her grandmother had made, eggshell with small Norwegian wild geese embroidered in deep greens and blues.

"That's the George Washington bridge," she said. He gave it a glance, turned to her, and said, "I want you to know I'm very grateful to you for taking me in, but don't put yourself out. I know it's New Year's Eve and you're . . ."

"It is the one night of the year I make a point of staying in," she said, a statement prepared in advance. She looked at him and he was not handsome. He had a long thin face with prominent cheekbones, more Mongolian than Irish, she thought, and a jutting chin. His hair looked black and his eyes looked black and he had some more to say.

"There's something I want to get straightened out. You remember what you said the last time?"

"No."

"Yes you do, Thoroughgood. You know damn well you called me a hypocrite. Well, that's the last thing I am, a hypocrite. And it makes me mad as hell."

"Good heavens! How belligerent you are, Ryan. Take your coat off and be civil."

"I'm glad you brought that up about being civil. You hit it exactly. I told you very carefully about my relationship to the church. I admitted I was an atheist by the time I was three years old. I brought you through a fairly subtle and actually quite private line of reasoning but you didn't have the courtesy—talking about being civil—to listen. You think there's something a little lower class about ambition. Well, there's this much to say about growing up in an Irish Catholic slum. You either get resigned or you spend every waking hour seeing how you can get sprung. You're right, I am ambitious. I'm politically ambitious. And I wouldn't have a chance in hell of winning anything in Massachusetts as Renegade Ryan. . . . You know, I don't even care about myself but I hate to see a good brain go sloppy. You can do better. . . . It really makes me . . . I'm no hypocrite, Erica. If you want to know about me, the first thing about me is that I'm a pragmatist."

She was wobbled by this bawling out, how serious he was, and didn't know which way to fall. At last she laughed, because her situation was funny, and said, "Okay, you're a pragmatist, but you're a pragmatist with a lot of crust."

He narrowed his black eyes at her for a moment, looked satisfied and unbuttoned his jacket.

Her family were having a few friends in for drinks and a light supper, she said, but it wasn't a formal party at all. He pulled out a street map of Manhattan from his hip pocket and said that he was going to walk across to Broadway, down Broadway to Times Square to watch the New Year in, continue south to the Village, turn east on 8th . . . his route was marked in red pencil.

"Walk? You don't seem to realize . . ."

"I figure on leaving here ten-thirty the latest. I'll just slip out quietly. The only problem would be to have a key to get in again."

Well, she didn't give a damn what he did, actually.

The guests came, they sidled about and drank. Her mother detached Frank and brought him along the walls to explain about the pictures, and later her grandmother limped up to ask him what law school he hoped to attend and he said the one offering the largest scholarship, and then her grandfather came round, put his hand on Ryan's shoulder, and asked him where he came from.

"I come from the working class and my ambition is to get out of it," Ryan said with a quick shy grin.

"Oh for crying out loud, Ryan, will you cut out the proletarian stuff," Erica snapped. "You're the only one in America who's class-conscious, except for the Communists, I suppose. He comes from Boston," she said to her grandfather primly.

"You are naïve, Erica, if you'll excuse my saying so about your granddaughter, Mr. Phillips. Everybody in America is class-conscious as hell."

"Are you a party member?" she asked in a mildly taunting voice. "Oh well, you wouldn't tell if you were anyway," she added indifferently.

"What's the matter with you, Erica?" her grandfather said sharply. "You insult Mr. Ryan—Frank, is it?—you insult Frank when you don't listen to what he says."

"Oh, she's all right, Mr. Phillips. I just get under her skin once in a while. She's complacent sometimes. The fact of the matter is I don't mind getting under her skin." Quick grin.

Later Frank told her that if she would like to go on his walk with him, he wouldn't mind, but she turned him down. At ten-thirty he was out the door, and it was after three when she heard the key in the lock. What kept her awake was the entirely fanciful notion that life was throwing a net over her and that she wouldn't struggle to get free. At midnight with the wind whipping at her window she could still hear the faint broken sound of bells tolling—the church at West End and 86th Street and St. Gregory the Great on 90th—she strained to make out which was which. They tolled for her all right . . . more tinkle than toll, if that wasn't ominous! And another thing she didn't like was the way he absolutely worshiped Hemingway . . . God, honestly, you'd think Ingrid Bergman in a sleeping bag would cure anyb—— . . . Actually, she had no feeling for or against poor innocent Ryan. She reminded herself again and again that she was perfectly free, perfectly free. Then what was it that left her mildly oppressed?

꿏

Chapter 4

The portents were bad but the year was good enough and perhaps the tolling was not for Erica. Perhaps for Billie. There was to be a June wedding and then in the spring it was called off. Billie had broken the engagement. Erica heard nothing more about Moriches until the eve of the Easter holidays of her senior year, 1948, when her grandfather telephoned her at school. Aunt Trudy was selling her house. He had to go out there on this matter but would wait for her if she liked. She was grateful to him.

She was terribly excited and nervous to see Billie again, to take the road from the station through the village down to the big house, to stand at the edge of the creek.

"You must be terribly excited about your trip, Ric. You have so loved Moriches," her mother said to her affectionately.

"Goodness, Ellen. I'm a little curious, but why would I be excited?" said the contrary girl who could not experience a strong emotion without throwing a cordon of denial around it. Now why was that? Alternately, she would pretend to a

strong emotion she didn't feel, Wilson's getting married for
an example. It was as if wherever she was, *that* couldn't be
okay. It was very nearly a reflex action saying she was someplace else.

The Sunday afternoon in April that they were to go was
raw and pouring.

"You ought to wear your muskrat coat, Ric. It'll be cold
as the devil out there," said Ellen. But Erica, chin up, said
nothing. She knew to the last bobby pin what she would
wear, cracked a raw egg on her wet head, and rinsed it
through her hair, an awful sensation. Later, before they left,
she sought out her mother, fell into her arms, began to cry,
and said, "Oh, I love you very much, Ellen."

"Dearest, dearest child," Ellen murmured, a mother once
more, strong and wise.

Ellen was wonderfully restored to sanity. Nothing specific
was ever said to Erica about it but she was allowed to understand from something her grandmother said about women
being prisoners of their biology that her mother had been
knocked off balance by the menopause but was now fine.
Wilson breezing through one week found occasion to say to
Erica that a love affair works wonders. It was a casual remark
but it froze her. It was beyond all plausibility, all likelihood,
because her mother was so old, forty-three. Romance, sex,
that sort of thing was strictly confined in Erica's mind to the
young. Sex in particular was their preserve. Especially was
this so with women. How unseemly, if this were true, that
Ellen . . . "Well, who is the man, Wilson?" "My God, child,
it's Caplan. You don't mean to say you don't know about this?
I'm sorry." "But what about Caplan's marriage?" "It didn't
work out, I suppose. She's Catholic, so there's to be no divorce." "I think you're crazy, Wilson."

Erica carried this around with her, a bundle of shame and
disgust until finally it was too heavy and she approached her
grandfather.

"I'm tormented by something I've heard, Grandpa. I don't

know who else to ask about it." He took off his reading glasses and attended to her, blinked, raised his brow in question, and one, two, three, four deep unbroken horizontal lines creased his forehead. When she was growing up she once read someplace that people with great minds had three unbroken lines when they wrinkled their foreheads, as with President Roosevelt. Four. Her grandfather had four.

"Has Ellen . . . fallen back in love with Mr. Caplan?"

"It seems so."

"Well are they . . . having a love affair?"

"That's my understanding."

"Well, why isn't it . . . morally reprehensible? I mean, first of all there's the wife. He did make his choice, after all. And second of all they hardly have the excuse of youth. I mean, you can't say they fell madly insanely in love and got swept off their feet. How could anyone say that?"

"Now, Ric . . ."

"You don't think she's wrong, do you? I can see it in your face, Grandpa. How can you condone such . . . I mean, I always think of you as being quite fastidious about people's behavior."

"Well, one hopes that people will be generous and kind and not make somebody else the victim of their private decisions. I don't see that either Ellen or Mr. Caplan is causing pain to anybody else. As I understand it, Mrs. Caplan seems to agree with her husband about their mutual incompatability, although she does not know of his liaison and perhaps would not take a cheerful view of it. So there is the dishonesty, of course. But sometimes people have to make a private accommodation with the rules of life; otherwise it is too barren, too bitter."

"Everybody wants to suspend the rules for himself."

"Add it up this way. Our poor Ellen is back on her feet, quite clearly her fine responsible self again. And let us presume that Mr. Caplan finds comfort and relief in his love for her. Of course, Mrs. Caplan is the unknown so we'll leave her at zero. It seems to pass the moral test of the greatest good for the greatest number."

"You're no Utilitarian. That's a thoroughly discreditable way of measuring value!" said Erica, who was taking Philosophy 323b.

"It's not thoroughly discreditable at all, Ric. Very little is. The hazards for the moral man are on both sides. One is more liable, I think, to become moralistic than to commit a seriously immoral act. And I don't think Ellen's act is seriously immoral."

Whether or not Mr. Caplan found comfort and relief with Ellen, Erica certainly drew them from her grandfather. To be pardoned from passing moral judgment against her mother on a matter explicitly sexual and therefore particularly sickening was an immense disburdenment. But as her soul lightened she felt her heart flood almost painfully with an engulfing love. At that very moment she had a glimpse through a crack into the bleak future of things where she saw, or thought she saw, that she would never love a man the way she loved her grandfather. It would be impossible.

Her grandfather was sixty-seven now, still feeling fine, although he said his carcass was creaking terribly and that he had a crick in his neck that hurt like the devil. He had a full head of hair, not very gray, and the only thing that had changed notably about him was that he had shrunken somewhat, so that as they walked beneath the high Pennsylvania Station skylight they seemed the same size—to Erica, both average.

"Everything's going to look a lot smaller to you in Moriches. D'you know that, Ric?"

"Yes, I've warned myself." Oh please don't let him die, she pleaded with the spirits in charge who had kept him alive so far. They got on their terribly disappointing train. It looked like an ordinary subway car with rows of seats in laquered yellow straw and a black ugly floor spotted with walked-on chewing gum. How diminishing for Moriches. And no chair car, no porters.

"The railroads aren't replacing their rolling stock," said Erica knowledgeably to impress her grandfather. In fact, she didn't know a thing about railroads and was superficially informed about every current thing, as Ryan was tireless in pointing out. Well, the hell with Ryan. "It just breaks my heart," she went on, "when I remember those lovely trips in my childhood in a parlor car that was all moss-green velvet and sparkling clean."

The rain rained and it was dark grey, still winter bare, out the window. Babylon, Bayshore, Islip . . . the same names called out. "You want to hear a limerick I know?" Erica asked her grandfather.

> "There's a girl out in Center Moriches
> Who kept all the neighbors in stitches
> She swam down to Islip
> And borrowed a dry slip
> And bicycled home without britches.

Like that?"

"It catches the grandeur of the area, without a question."

They were passing pine scrub, miles and miles of it. "Grandpa, I think I remember this!" she said, and her grandfather took one bleak look at the bleak scrub and went to sleep. Scrub interminable. Billie would probably look like a million dollars. Erica believed she herself had a madonna like composure but would Billie notice? It had stopped raining by Mastic, the last station but one, and then finally the whistle blew and they were slowing. Her grandfather led her through the now nearly empty car. Almost nobody left to go all the way out to Montauk. She couldn't wait to see them, and was suddenly too shy to be seen. Down the steps and one swift look around, and *nobody*. A second slower look at nothing but the empty station driveway—so ill-kept, with straggly dead grass poking through the pebbles and the paint of the stationhouse aged to the color of lentil soup. How they let the place go. Nobody at all but a lone taxi. And where could they be, and how they let her down. "What'll we do, Grandpa?"

"We'll take the taxi," he said, not flustered. "I've got a riddle for you. Do you know the difference between the Panama Canal and Mrs. Van Brink? The first is a busy ditch and the second a dizzy bitch! Like that?"

"No! I'm laughing at you." He took good care of her. She watched from the taxi window and remembered almost everything, the little department store where they sold rubber beach balls in the summer and the bank, but how dreary the village was without the leaves on the trees. Then they were so quickly in the driveway of the big half-familiar house, and then at the door, and "Oh, Effie! Do you know who I am?"

"Why, Erica honey, you aren't changed one bit. You the same sweet brown-eyed little girl. . . . What you doing here so early? Miz Van Brink tole Billie meet the 8:22."

"There isn't an 8:22 until Memorial Day, Effie. You look beautiful! Exactly the same. Do you remember my grandfather, Mr. Phillips?" And Erica hugged Effie and looked past her where the carpets and pictures were gone.

"What is all that commotion out there, Effie? Must I get up?" called out exactly the same querulous voice she had known those years ago, and Erica slipped off to the doors of the double parlor. There without a doubt was Aunt Trudy, grown much fatter, bent over a game of checkers with a withered Uncle Anton, she having no intention whatever of getting up, not even lifting her head. They sat, the two of them, as though they were in the last scene of a play in the twin rooms that had cluttered Erica's mind from childhood, twin rooms grown larger from being stripped, bare windows, walls, floor. The ghosts of chairs and sofas covered by white sheets lined the shadows, while in the middle of the empty floor a bridge table was set up for their checkers with a gooseneck lamp to light them, its long cord wriggling off to a socket in the wall. Uncle Anton had added a muffler to his neck and a golf hat to his ancient-looking head. Aunt Trudy wore a white summer coat with a large red fox collar.

"Aunt Trudy, we're here. "It's Erica." Talk about commotion!

"What time is it? How did they get here so soon? Can you beat it, a grown woman! And how unreliable the trains are! Tony, look at her. Would you recognize our own little Erica? And your grandfather says you are off to law school . . . a Portia!—'I never shall repent for doing good, nor shall not now—' Portia!" Aunt Trudy had been in the Cypress Hills-Stratford Repertory Theatre *before* she had been pulled from the stage by heady passion.

"How *are* you, Uncle Anton?"

"Bad."

"That's because he gives in to himself," said Aunt Trudy, and then to Erica's grandfather she said, "You see? Do I lie? Do I exaggerate? Do you want whisky and soda or shall I make you a nice dry martini with a twist of lemon peel? And you, Erica, I bet you are anxious to take a look at your old sister, whisky for you?" Up hill and down dale they went with her.

"I can't wait to see Billie, Aunt Trudy. Where is she?"

"Half the time I don't know, Mr. Phillips," she said, as if her grandfather had asked. "She's wild as the devil, that one. It's because I've had to raise her alone. Ah, Erica, if I had not lost your poor father. Together we might. . . . The first one, *c'était un marriage de convenance, vous savez*, Mr. Phillips? But Tom, Tom was a love match. My life came to an end when—pull those two chairs over, Effie . . . just *take* the sheets off and *pull*—my heart drowned with his. I don't complain . . ." she complained, and all the while she talked she was prestidigitating, whisking bottles and glasses from under the sheets in the shadows, producing lovely cheeses, English biscuits, doing what she was meant to do. Always to Erica her Aunt Trudy seemed a disorderly rosy peasant with her fair hair wound in a coronet, somebody Heidi might have run into in the Alps.

"We could not get Gouda, we could not get Brie, we could not get Apfenszel right through the war. That's how I lost my health. It ruined my metabolism, that Wisconsin stuff," said Uncle Anton.

"You don't know what you're talking about, Tony. Why would the doctor put you on a low-carbohydrate diet? This is what I have to put up with, Mr. Phillips, from one end of the day to . . ."

"Where is Billie, Aunt Trudy?" Erica asked, tasting an old bad taste.

"Oh, Erica, you won't recognize her! She's a real heartbreaker, that one. Between the two of them, Tony and Billie . . . that's why I have to sell, Mr. Phillips. My nerves can't take it. Billie, with that will-she, won't-she marriage last year. I can't tell you what it cost me, money I could not get back . . . a fancy deposit at the old Tearose Inn . . ."

"Who is buying this house?" Erica cut ahead.

"So Billie is at this minute probably on her way to the station . . ." Aunt Trudy crossed back.

"A nuclear physicist from the Brookhaven Laboratory," said Uncle Anton. "We're damned lucky. Imagine! What a wilderness! And then they decide it's just the place to set up the most advanced scientific center. If it wasn't for that we couldn't have given this place away."

"How can you say such a thing, Tony! Three acres of waterfront property . . ."

And then finally in the doorway was Billie the knockout,

and whatever there had been about her to cause Erica to melt with love was right there again as alive as deep. She had a warm immediate grin with a lot of affection and a little mockery in it, perhaps it was that. People had always remarked two things in Billie: her common touch—her affection was really very democratic, she didn't parcel it out according to your rank—and the other thing they always said was what a good sport. She was certainly built for it, taking the meaning the other way, and dressed for it in blue jeans and a man's shirt. Front to back she was long and slim, but face on her body was angular, nearly husky. Nothing of the parts was remarkable, only the whole. And on top of everything was her adorable head in its own style, her hair close-cropped, carefully uncombed and kept golden out of the same old bottle, probably. She had the same snub nose and a bridge of pale bewitching freckles and that breezy way with her, that easy spendthrift confidence, that everybody was bound to be crazy about her, that being liked wasn't her problem. She looked to Erica as though *problems* weren't her problem. *Still*, after all this time.

When the dust had settled, or actually before, Aunt Trudy said, "What a lady Erica is beside you, Billie!"

"You look terrific, Erica," said generous Billie. "Like a model, like a model Modigliani would use. I'm not kidding. The more I look at you the more I can see Modigliani. Of course, you could take all your beautiful clothes off and stretch out on the couch and then we could be sure." Oh Billie!

From the time that Erica knew she was to make this visit, she had daydreamed circles around Moriches, as though the middle of Moriches, once she finally got there, contained a great surprise. She had paid particular mind to the entrance she would make, the figure she would cut; and the event had to fall short. But not the dinner, not the roast duck and dumplings, the rosé wine and the Sacher torte still a touch

warm. Still, the evening was a touch boring. Erica ate greed-
ily like a child.

What extraordinary person she thought Billie was bound
to make of herself she had not specifically imagined. It had
hung in limbo.

Right through to dessert Billie in the flesh seemed envia-
bly at one with herself. Yes, she liked Vassar although she
was just skidding by, she said, hunching her shoulders
against the wrath of her mother. "And no wonder, with
every weekend in New Haven!" said her mother on cue.
"Good Time Charlie, that one. When do you think you're
going to settle down and take life seriously, my dear?"

"I'm going to put it off as long as I possibly can," said her
dear, not rudely, but meaning it. Erica, needing to account
for her own significance, cut herself an intellectual figure,
coming out rather too successfully upright. She would have
liked to fray her edges but Aunt Trudy had a relish for setting Billie against Portia. It all sailed over Billie's head, the
way Billie seemed to sail through life itself, like a kite blown
by every happy wind. A kite on a very long string. And that
was how Erica saw Billie, whooping around the sky having
a grand time, while down underneath across the flat land on
a straight track she saw herself clackety-clack, the thoroughgood express—always reliable, on time—not asking, Why?
Not daring.

After dinner Billie and Erica curled into the white sheet
of one sofa at the end of one parlor while Erica's grandfather
and Aunt Trudy bent over legal papers at the farther end of
the other. Uncle Anton had been sent to bed. It was cold
as the devil because of Aunt Trudy's camellia bush. Almost
immediately the half-sisters joined their lives. Erica, hovering above the subject of that broken engagement, suddenly
dove down upon it like a gull to the sea only on a tender
mission: "Did you fall out of love, was that it?"

"Jesus, I just got scared. I don't think love had anything to do with it. I couldn't stand . . . life closing in on me that way. Everybody mobilizing. It was like total war, and the single objective was my unconditional surrender . . . do you know what I'm talking about? I mean, I just had to be free. Oh God, I don't fool myself for a minute that they're not going to get me in the end. I know I'm going to be married and have children, and I think that's right. . . . Do you think I'm crazy? Do you ever have that feeling?" Billie wanted to know. Answers crowded in upon Erica.

"I have every feeling," she said finally.

"Do you believe in destiny?"

"Destiny? Oh no, Billie, no. No, no. You don't mean, 'There's a divinity that shapes our ends, rough-hew them how we will'—that sort of destiny?"

"If I ever have a daughter I'm going to name her Moira."

"Do you mean that you know, on the one hand, that you're entirely free to refuse to go down a certain path, say, and you don't want to go down it. But your sixth sense tells you in the end you will . . . that fate without any reason, without any purpose, sort of hypnotizes you . . . almost for the hell of it?"

"That's exactly what I mean, exactly. Do you feel that way too?"

"No . . . I mean intellectually I'm simply unable to take a teleological view." Erica retreated behind her vocabulary. She had trouble being honest with herself, that's all. She faded in and out of knowing this. At one point during the evening Aunt Trudy was describing somebody to her grandfather in a voice that cut across the rooms—"but there isn't an honest bone in his body!"

"That's my body!" Erica cried out to herself.

Chapter 5

Erica was persuaded to stay on in Moriches for a day or two longer. After her grandfather returned to the city, Billie with great good nature trailed her through the gray drizzle down to the creek where there was no boat, and then back up the road where she half remembered every house, every tree, to the end where there still was the iron gate of the Little Sisters of Charity. Billie said it was deserted in winter, that they could get in by a break in the hedge. They wriggled through like little children, and were bound together in love by raindrops down their necks and by scratches. Erica had never been on these grounds. Right in the middle of them sat the mother house, unexpectedly stark, uncomforted, without the leaf screen and the lilac hedge. Trespassing against her, the girls walked along the driveway round to the front and on to the great porch. All the windows were boarded against the winter. They sat on the top step. In front of them beyond the flat span of grey lawn was very nearly infinity, the mild bay rippling off imprecisely to the whitened sky. Erica, exerting an effort to bathe in the memories of her childhood, found that she could not attend to the past at all.

"Were you really in love with that man?" she asked Billie.

"With Sam? I was crazy about him. He's around. We hang out with the same crowd. He'll probably be there tonight, up at Quogue. He's the best dancer I ever danced with in my life but I don't dance with him any more. We just give a nod, that's all."

"Are you very unhappy?"

"I'm very *happy!* 'Don't fence me in!'—that's my song. If I don't like where I am I just pick up my marbles and go. That sounds terrible, doesn't it? Do you remember when we were little you were the good girl and I was the bad girl, but really I'm not bad. I just don't want to be pinned down . . . it scares me." She smiled her magic smile, and on the instant her faults dissolved. Lean and long-armed, her hair curly from the damp, a Greek youth, she seemed simply beyond reach of the intimidation Erica knew.

"You look like Hermes resting from racing around the world with his messages," said Erica, sighing for her own disharmonious self. Sufficient unto Billie's day were the pleasures thereof. Not Erica's. Erica banked upon the deep and passionate future. She saw precious few signs of its imminence.

"I'd rather look like Hermes than a housewife, I'll tell you that," said Billie. "I don't want to settle down yet. I'm just not ready. Are you ready?"

"No, I'm not ready," Erica said and paused, and the truth made a little sortie to the front. "On the other hand, it would be just as true to say I'm ready as hell. Sometimes I think I bide my time with every other living thing I do until . . . I'd just like to fall madly in love."

"Yes, it's very nice."

"Billie . . . did you ever go all the way . . . with anybody, with Sam?"

"No. I mean I don't have any principles about it. . . . Did you? With your guy at Harvard?"

"He's not . . . oh no . . . God."

Billie was straight with herself, absolutely straight, thought crooked Erica. Not under orders from anybody. Well who is it, she wondered, that I am always taking orders from? Whom do I obey? Suppose I refused, she proposed to herself. What would it come to? A mutiny against nobody?

Billie drove Erica to a party in Quogue that evening at the summer home of an American who had his own oil in the Near East. For this party Billie needed ten minutes to put herself together, Erica the afternoon. It was an amazing house set at the edge of a pond, the outside a proper weather-beaten shingle, its long porch strung with Chinese lanterns. But step inside and you were in a great room rich and exotic hung with oriental rugs, carrot-colored, mud-brown, blues, and there were beaded curtains weaving and clicking and brass trays and silver things in dark corners. A lot of people were milling and drinking or dancing to Cole Porter's *Kiss Me Kate* on the phonograph. They were all ages and rich but not exotic. Ella Fitzgerald was singing "But I'm always true to you darling in my fashion, Yes I'm always true to you darling in my way," and a man in a white dinner jacket sort of brushed by them as they took their measure in the doorway and said, in a sardonic way, "That's you, Billie."

Billie was easy, friendly with lots of people, wouldn't dance yet, said this was her sister, and looked wonderful in a white jersey dress that hung upon her angularity, making her fairly flat chest seem alluring as hell. Erica, in a blue-black silk dress with a neck that scooped to rounder effect, looked alluring as hell too, but she couldn't feel sure of it and her manner was a little stand-offish. Moreover, two alien things took her by surprise, the one causing her to mount her defenses, the other allowing them to collapse. The first was This Much Money, or, rather, This Kind of money. This sort of people, politically immoral. . . . The gossip of the evening, and it wasn't greeted by a hoot, was that their host the oil man, whichever one he was, had just signed over ten thousand dollars to support the candidacy of Governor Dewey for the Republican nomination in July. None of the proper nouns in that rumor was the language of respect in Erica's world, no number like that its currency. Here was the enemy. Up went her chin. And wouldn't Ryan have a star-spangled fit in a crowd like this! She was a guest. Of course there was nothing she could say here. The second thing to which she was unaccustomed was a dry martini. It was rancid, unbelievably unswallowable, looked like motor oil, and tried her character very fittingly. Among the Yahoos she never flinched.

Some time or other, *some time or other,* she had sunk for a rest among the lovely flowered pillows of a raffia settee, and had turned to whomever it was sitting on it too, and said with good cheer: "I bet I'm the only one in this whole damn room who's going to vote for Henry Agard Wallace!"

"I don't want to crowd you out of your glory, dearie, and I don't want to take your money, but *I'm* going to vote for Henry Agard Wallace *several times.*"

She gave a large blink to her eyes, not her grandfather's granddaughter for nothing, and instantly her couch-sharer became a prince and she said, "I guess I have just fallen hopelessly in love with you."

It was only a sample of their clever repartee that night, and through the good offices of gin Erica would recall very little of it. In the matter of love she had been, of course, hanging heavy from the bough, very ripe to fall, and now she fell flat on her face. The rich are different, said Hemingway. Yes, they have money, said Hemingway. No, they are really different, Erica thought disloyally, and the ones that are blond and need haircuts and are handsome and careless usually are in the habit of looking right through the subtle and superior Ericas, making their beeline for the beautiful Billies. But here, miraculously, was one who had stopped before her. So attractive was his lazy drawl, his indifference to the way his jacket hunched and his suspenders showed, that very soon it really didn't matter whom he was going to vote for. If the truth were in Erica, she would have told herself straightaway that this was certainly bound to be Billie's Sam but the truth wasn't in her. Nor in him.

"I don't dance," said the most terrific dancer, "but I walk. Let's go for a walk." When they had gone down the drive way he turned her around by the shoulders to look back at the house with the light and the music bursting from the windows and he said, "They're on the *Titanic*. They haven't an idea in hell that they're all through. Boom!" he boomed, and wiped out her enemy. She let herself lean against his chest for one moment and he kissed the top of her head, and she asked what did he do? Do! He was just taking a goddam rest period, he just needed time to think, for Chrissake, which his old man had never taken the time to do, nor would he know what the hell it was all about, thinking! In fact, he was trying to write. He'd got through the war business and Princeton and now he was just taking a breather. It wasn't all that goddam restful. He'd be sitting in his room with his feet up on the typewriter and there'd be his mother in the doorway looking at him with tears in her eyes. "They think writing is malingering, the whole bunch of them. No, actually I'm not being fair. They approve of *some* writers. They think D. H. Lawrence did a terrific job in Arabia."

Erica laughed and then said, "Lawrence just fascinates me . . . Gudrun and Ursula in *Women in Love*—I admire them enormously." Chiefly she admired them for their being irresistible and eye-catching in their red and green and yellow stockings, and also she admired herself for wading through the whole boring book. "Is Lawrence the kind of writer that you want to . . ."

"Hemingway." Hemingway? My God, the fights she and Ryan had about that precious Lady Brett. But now she hadn't the least inclination to argue. Now . . . now she was Lady Brett—ha! But this guy was *not* Jake. "Who are you?" she asked him when it was about time to leave.

"I am the proverbial third son in a family of three sons. The n'er-do-well, but of course I will get to marry a princess —the last thing I want to do on a list running to twelve pages single-space: marry. My oldest brother was destined for the ministry, but he . . . and my second brother for the law, and so that left medicine for me. They're a bit short in imagination at home."

"What does your father do?"

"Nothing. He's on Wall Street. What does yours?"

"He drowned in Moriches Inlet when I was eleven."

"You're Billie's sister!" He seemed really surprised.

"You're Billie's Sam!" So did she seem.

"I'm my own man, dearie," he said quietly from the bottom of his throat.

Afterward in the car, Billie couldn't wait to ask Erica what she thought of him.

"The fact of the matter is," Erica heard herself say, "I hadn't the least idea it was Sam almost until the end of the evening."

"I suppose you didn't talk about me at all?" Billie was shy about this.

"We talked politics mostly. My God, he really is a renegade. What does his family make of him?"

"They don't understand him at all. They just think he's weak."

Erica was delivered over to a private excitement about Sam deriving from nothing substantial and promising no future, but she couldn't sleep for it. Nor could Billie, who settled herself next morning on the foot of Erica's bed to talk. Billie said she was preoccupied with Sam and couldn't shake it. Open, honest, and reprehensible Billie swore she didn't want to marry, but the idea that Sam might take up with somebody else made her jealous as hell. She knew she was unreasonable, and besides, she was certain he hadn't been dating at all, but on the other hand he was a very horny guy and sooner or later he was going to find somebody else.

"That's when I lose my resolution," she said with easy confidence to Erica, who made sympathetic murmuring sounds. "I know a lot of girls who'd grab the chance . . . and I don't kid myself that his money and all that don't count . . . but then I remind myself, do I want to live in Edinburgh for the next four years, and then I want to scream with joy for getting out of it. I'm out, thank God, I'm out!"

"Edinburgh?"

"He's going to medical school. Didn't he tell you that? So that's four years absolutely shot, absolutely out of things, and then another three years of God knows where for internship and residency—that's seven years. Seven years! I'd feel like an indentured slave. I've had enough trouble sticking out my time at Vassar. New York is an obsession with me, Ric. I've just got to get there and be free, walk down Fifth, go out every night without having to report who it was and where we went and what time I got in . . . I've just got to be free of the colonial mentality. It's from too much living in the outposts of empire. Moriches, Bridgeport, Poughkeepsie—Jesus, what a list. How can anybody expect me to add Edinburgh? Of course, you've lived in New York all your life, Ric. Edinburgh might sound romantic and foreign to you, not like Devil's Island."

"I always envied you for living in Moriches, for belonging to it," said Erica, and as for Edinburgh it sounded marvelous.

"Oh, I love Moriches, and now I'm going to love New York. That's all! I feel great. It helps me to talk this out, Ric. Sometimes I lose my bearings."

Aunt Trudy was interested to have Billie lose her bearings and asked at lunch whether poor Sam was there last night.

"He's still carrying the torch, I bet you!" she said.

"She's well rid of him," said Uncle Anton. "No backbone."

"Just lift her little finger, that's all she'd have to do," Aunt Trudy said with a small sigh, the only size sigh she dared, evidently. Billie turned on her mother angrily and said she thought it was understood that her mother had cut that out!

And by evening Erica was on the train back to New York. The train rocked, she was breathing short breaths to its rhythm. Her mind slid back to her night with Sam and forward to their meeting again in the most surprising ways, depending upon many marvelous coincidences. She was swept by exhilaration, by joy. The unreality of her fantasy was no trouble at all. Her fantasies had always been unreal, everybody's were. But this one had a true core. She didn't dream up Sam. Sam was his own man, as he said himself.

Chapter 6

The cold wet weather of Moriches gave way to a forerunning of spring in New York. The mild air was a cosmic sign. Erica smiled and nodded, took long walks, and was feeling beautiful. All this over nothing, she knew, and she hummed. Her confidence swelled to an immense size. The real Sam and his real indifference to her were not germane. Before she left for her final months at Smith she announced to her family at dinner that she had made a large decision: she would not go to law school. The law was something she had headed for without ever having a true sense of vocation, she told them, with a shy smile to her grandfather. For a wonder, everybody heard her very respectfully. Her mother suggested she might want to go into art history after all. Her grandmother thought she was born to teach. Wilson and Muffie were visiting for Easter, Muffie enormous in her seventh month. They lived in San Diego, where he was a civilian dispatcher for the Navy. He did not say, "How about becoming a sailor?" You had to give him credit for that. Muffie said, "Every girl wants her own home."

Erica returned to school a new woman—derailed. To her best friends she was oblique about Sam, for want of any other way to be. Look! I'm different, am I not? she said to them and they said Yes. The proof of the pudding was that she cut several classes and did very little work. Virtue was rewarded because she could skid home free on the past achievements of her previous studious, attentive, thorough-good now-abandoned self. She did not reward virtue back but put it behind her with other childish things. That ought to cheer Ryan up. Ryan! Her honors thesis, which she had not finished writing, was a defense of the intentions of the New Deal legislation to effect a more equitable distribution of wealth. Ryan had looked over her first draft and said her gutwork was good but her philosophy was bankrupt. "You have a child's view of the world," he said. "It's amazing. You think you can pick people up in distress and kiss them and make them all better." "I don't know what you're talking about, Ryan," she said dismissively. But it was not easy to dismiss Ryan, that long gangle.

Last fall after he had begun law school she went to visit him in Cambridge. They had been walking amicably enough along the river when he suddenly blew up. Afterward he said it was because she was outlining a plan to ease the lot of sharecroppers by sending their children to Harvard. "It's inexcusable!" he snapped. "You are so simple-mindedly mechanical in your thinking. You just never have quite made it into the nineteenth century, never quite caught up with Darwin and Freud."

"Freud! I don't care about their sex problems!"

"You've got a Sunday-school mentality. You just swallowed the whole dumb story of life. You're the star in a morality play." He was exasperated.

"I never went to Sunday school in my life! My family were

pedigreed atheists when yours were still painting themselves blue and running around beyond the pale. And you're still beyond the pale, Ryan!"

But he had the last word, whatever it was. His crack about the morality play was not far from the mark. Intuitively she acted as though she had been born into the leading role in a ritual drama that depended heavily upon her for stage managing, for directing, for filling many of the necessary roles, and for a lot of the dialogue,

> As if her whole vocation
> Were endless imitation.

There was a large cast. Sometimes people made up their own lines and sometimes she did not like that. She had brought Ryan in off the streets to be the stand-in, the *temporary* stand-in, for the hero. Heroines cannot after all wander around unattended. But he'd been playing the part for more than a year and he thought it was his. No sir.

The new Erica was becoming a trifle restless inside her new self after living through a couple of weeks pointlessly, without any goal, purpose, direction, without any way to measure herself and find she was good. The original image of the original Sam was now limp, all the stuffing worked out of it. She had had one unsatisfactory conversation on the phone with Ryan in which she told him she had withdrawn her applications to law school and about needing time to Find Herself, an alternative pursuit currently chosen by a few war veterans and some sultry girls at school who were reading *The Prophet*. Not, of course, that Erica would fall for something like *The Prophet*. Ryan was predictably unsympathetic and said, "All right, be trivial! Spend your life being trivial! There's plenty of scope for you!"

It took days to shrug him off, but by the end of the week her pulse was barely beating from any of the late causes. After Sunday dinner she ambled out with her friend Mary to sit on the curb in the quad beneath the Weeping Siberian Peatree, a very ordinary-looking small bush. All the trees at Smith had their names on them. Both girls were groggy, both tilted their faces toward the early spring sun and smoked a cigarette preliminary to settling down in the reading room of the library for a deep sleep. "Probably," observed Erica, "probably a white convertible Buick is the most petty-bourgeois symbol of them all. Watch that one scrape its fenders." And they snorted as it inched its outsized way around the quad when Erica said, "My God, Mary, it's Sam."

It was handsome Sam, collar open in a grey-blue Shetland sweater, pretty pastel Sam—not loud primary Ryan always looking like Christmas, like the Italian flag—it was casual ambling Sam, who said, memorably, "Hello, dearie, I didn't know you'd be so easy to find" to Erica, with no lipstick, who was yanking at her skirt, who was smirking awfully, possibly giggling, but still conscious. This-is-Mary-Jason-this-is-Sam-Ives, hi. Hi, and almost immediately good Mary says she'd got to do her paper. Erica was wide awake now, and there was to be no nap, no by your leave about the movies Mary, do-you-mind?

If Erica had to ask herself why she had stopped in her tracks, abandoned direction, thrown over the law, she would have had plenty of good answers. The touch of old Billie and the touch of new Sam had stirred an inchoate impatience with this eternal preparing, this never getting there, this forever waiting on the porch until it was time. She had come home from Moriches finished with getting ready; she was ready. The initial bounce this produced in her spirits was, however, quieting down to a dribble, and if Sam, or a reasonable facsimile, hadn't shown up she would have been all right, old Ric, would have lapsed back into being dogged, accomplished, and upstanding. But there, thank God, he was, and at the first sight of his fair face she was prescient, saw the whole thing laid out, and was glad to the bone for the chance to swop the future for the present.

He looked at once younger and older than she remembered, in a way like a handsome baby, Holbein's infant King Edward VI, or on the other hand like Van Johnson in that Saroyan movie about the Armenians, a sweet ten-year-old boy-face, now thirty, weathered and with a touch of rue. In fact he was twenty-three. He'd got hold of this German camera, he said, and he was heading up toward Canada, taking his time, catching the spring through his lens as it was about to break out hour by hour, through New England—like Monet, painting his haystack, he said, and Rouen Cathedral. "Do you know that our museum has a Rouen Cathedral?" she asked, but he skipped on, was heading for the Mohawk Trail, he said, when he just remembered that she was at Smith, and how about being his guide for a couple of hours?

They drove with the top down over the Calvin Coolidge Bridge looking for a road down to the river, and he said he had a bellyful of the woman business, that he just wanted a plain ordinary goddam sensible human being to talk to, "meaning you, Ric." He tooketh away a lot but gaveth back a little. She pulled on her heavy sweater and flung herself into sensible friendship.

April was the kindest month this year, this afternoon the loveliest. They walked along the Ox-bow through the still-bare woods with sweaters enough for the top of them, while their feet sank into old snow and skidded on old ice. Sam, with his camera, light meter, and other photographic equipment hanging from his neck, did not strangle. By squatting, by climbing trees and hanging upside down, he intended to take by surprise the ubiquity of it all. Erica—who kept saying things like "Oh God, isn't it beautiful!"—was faintly aware that she wasn't deeply stirred by spring waking on the Connecticut River, as she hadn't been really moved to be back at the creek in Moriches, or by actually sitting on the steps of the mother house. She had tried but she failed. It was as though for reasons of emotional economy she had to play out these acts without scenery. Sam said he was seriously thinking of doing a book of photographs on seasons, maybe following the spring north from, say, Mississippi through to the Alaskan tundra, if he had only thought of it by February. But he could take the fall and come south with it. Erica wondered what about his writing, what about medical school, but didn't ask. It was quite late when he returned her to her door and said if she were game for another round he would pick her up at noon. "At noon?" "I sleep in the morning because I don't sleep at night." "You aren't going to have one dawn in your book!"

The next day, with the weather holding, they drove up into the Berkshires, where it was still altogether winter. Oh, if only time would stop, the foolish virgin sighed to herself, borrowing the sigh. If time had stopped she'd be stuck forever on another threshold. This friendship, as it advanced through the hours of two days, was resting upon a wobbly presumption of their intellectual affinity, a soul-searching they had in common. In a silence that lasted too long, Erica, uneasy, would dart out into the world for a subject, a robin tugging at a worm, their mutual interest in politics: "In Massachusetts we've got to get thousands of signatures merely to have his name on the ballot! Every afternoon next week I've promised to ring doorbells . . ."

"Hell, where I come from, pahdner, ring that doorbell and you're a dead man. We shoot Commies first and ask questions later. Why, my old man'd consider it a duty and an honor to turn in his own mother for a Communist, witness her putting Russian dressing on her lettuce."

"What does he say about your voting for Wallace?"

"He says if I do he'll cut me off without a cent."

"My God, Sam, what are you going to do?"

"I'm going to exercise my inviolable right to vote for whom I goddam well please." And he tramped off, right out of the subject, his interest exhausted.

Sam was indefatigable about his picture-snapping, and Erica guessed that photography was for him a branch of physical education, a terrific outdoorsy thing to do until you could get back on the slopes again. Unathletic Erica grew tired, chilled, and even a trifle bored tracking after this man with his muscles and his giant steps. You could hardly have a satisfactory conversation with someone's back. Then when they'd gotten to a fine scratchy straw-colored field, by a great piece of luck his film ran out. And while he fussed and strode off, his arms flapping over the waste of this beautiful bowl they were in without a lens to see it through, the black hills rimming it, the sky a deepening blue, Erica, the supplies carrier, wrapped herself in one of the supplies, an army blanket, and fitted herself into a furrow against the now perishing cold.

She really was in a dark blue-violet furrow so that when he looked around he couldn't see her at first. She lay there swaddled tight and narrow, the whole sky above to stare into with x-ray eyes, while the straw was poking into her scalp, and then Sam came and stood over her, a giant, dark blue too, and laughed. He enjoyed finding her in a furrow very much.

"Do you know what you look like?" she asked him. "A fertility daemon."

"Good God, who is he?"

"Well he's good, but not quite a god."

"I thought daemons were evil," he said, and crouched on the next furrow.

"Oh that's not true! That's a typical Christian distortion.

'O Antony, stay not by his side.
Thy demon, that thy spirit which keeps thee, is
Noble, courageous, high, unmatchable,
Where Caesar's is not . . .'

That's what the soothsayer says to Antony. Greek daemons
are very good indeed, although they have a hard time. You
may not be up to it."

"What do I have to do?" he asked her.

"A lot of leaping. You have to

'Leap for full jars, and leap for fleecy flocks,
And leap for fields of fruit, and for hives to bring
increase.'

It's a spring rite, you see. You're the center of the most glorious festival of the year."

"Oh, if it's leaping for fleecy flocks, I'm up to it! Don't
worry about that."

"Well, that's just the beginning. First you leap and then
you fall. The gist of the problem is that the old winter must
die and everything's got to come up green and fertile and the
best way to do that, they thought, is to cut you up in countless little pieces and scatter your flesh over the fields and
then plow you under. This makes for a very promising harvest."

"You're right. I'm not up to it."

"Now wait a minute. That's the bad part."

"I agree. What happens next?"

"Loud lamentations! The messenger brings the news about
what's become of you and there is a great deal of weeping
and wailing. You like that, don't you?"

"I don't like it enough."

"And then epiphany! You get resurrected, flesh and spirit,
and you are top dog until the next spring. I grant you there
are drawbacks. For one thing, it's repetitive, but after all

it's very flattering. They only choose the most admired, handsome youth," she said, beaming up into his admired, handsome face. Then the daemon slipped to his knees beside her, lifted her head and shoulders, looked at her eyes, her nose, her mouth, and kissed her a long kiss. The kiss released her passion, the single thing she devoutly wished they might have in common.

"I didn't want to do that," he said, after they had come apart, and he looked at her soberly. She wondered whether he felt he had broken some kind of contract with the beauty queens he was used to. She could not pretend an answering regret, and perhaps he kissed her again from kindness to cover her very vulnerability.

❀

Chapter 7

Erica, lying in her furrow wrapped to the ears, could not have been more innocent in spite of her success in invoking her daemon. But it was very cold so the daemon and his lady lumbered clumsily off, all their equipment bumping together, to the car, where they fell into each other's arms again. It was in a car pulled over to the side of the road that she felt a loss of innocence. It was not the classical loss of innocence because the idea of "going all the way" was absolutely beyond Erica's courage or ambition and probably beyond Sam's. However, her self-respect was based in large measure upon self-control. And while she might yield up to passion in an open field, romance is vulgarly reduced when one is half-buttoned in the cramped space of a car watching for the headlights of a patrolling cop. Up to a point she abandoned herself to her lust, to Sam's lust, but not without shame, and altogether without humor. A long time later they were exhausted and starving.

Back in town over dinner they talked about photography

and how Sam would go off next day at noon to Quebec and out to the Bay of Fundy to catch the spring bore. "Your face is so serious," he said, in the nice voice he might use to comfort a worried child. "Don't you know that I want to come back this way? And it will give you a week to get your thesis done." Thereupon her face cleared. They talked about a lot of things but they never mentioned their underlying single-minded obsession and they never said they loved, and Sam had her back by her ten-fifteen deadline.

It was more than a week before Sam came back. It was nine days, and he had a nine-day beard and he said, "See! Here I am. A bad penny. I told you I'd turn up again." Casual, without an apology for leaving her tormented those last two days.

"Some spring!" he said. "In Montreal I was nearly buried in a blizzard. Well, I thought, I'm not out of my mind. The hell with a blanket roll. So I holed up in the Mount Royal for five days."

"Five days was the blizzard?"

"Oh hell no. I just liked walking around reading the French signs. Like Paris. You know, when the war was over and I was waiting to be demobbed I couldn't get over the seriousness with which those people spoke French, even in emergencies. They were superb. They really had guts."

"What about the bore?"

"Well, actually, dearie, a bore is a bore is a bore."

"Oh Sam!" He went on with this and she laughed, but she was hurt that he could have dawdled so in Canada. Later, once more in the dark and once more in the car, she was restored by his mindless hunger for her. They went something beyond kissing. She was wildly excited to feel that his hands had to touch her breast, that his mouth—and then Sam would plead with her to come up to his room for the night. Mary would cover for her. "They don't have bed checks, for God's sake." But the thing was too appalling, she couldn't possibly, and she would say, "Oh God, Sam, it's just four weeks until graduation. I just can't get expelled now, my poor family . . ."

Next Sam went back to New York, where in winter everybody lived, and next she went down for the weekend.

They never spoke of Billie, but Billie, if she did not preside over their relationship, had something to do with the delimiting of its boundaries. She kept them in hiding. Whether it was because of their unselfish concern for her feelings, or because Sam didn't want to appear cast off, or because Erica didn't want him handed down, it was their unspoken intention that neither Erica's poor family nor Sam's rich one was to get wind of it. This made her time in New York a bit of a trick for Erica, who paid scant attention to anybody at home and only slept in her own bed.

Her mother said, "For goodness sake, Ric, you weren't in until all hours. Is Ryan in town?"

"Oh Ellen, Ryan and I are all through," said Erica from her heart.

"Oh my darling, I'm so sorry. Then I suppose he won't be coming for your graduation?"

"God, yes, he's coming."

"I see. . . . Then he doesn't know he's all through?"

"Well, he's working his head off to get on the Law Review. I don't want to bring the thing up now."

"What's the name of his successor?"

"Sam."

"Sam what?"

"Just Sam for now. Ellen, I'm sorry. Maybe I need a little mystery in my life."

There was to be a wedding that Saturday in New York at which, Sam rather casually announced, he would make an appearance. It was his cousin Geraldine, a first cousin, and he promised his mother he'd drop in at the reception anyway. Sherry's, he thought it was at Sherry's. His mother

was family-minded. Erica's spirits sank to be without him
for those hours but no, hell no, she had to come too, where
would be the fun without her?

"I am going to give you an alias," he said. "I am going to
introduce you to everybody as just plain Lady Brett. They're
all illiterates. There won't be one goddam person there who
isn't delighted to think he is meeting a member of the Brit-
ish nobility. Of course, we couldn't pull it off, Ric, if you
weren't noble and elegant. But you are noble and elegant,"
he said seriously to her. In their endless talking together
they didn't use the words of love. Love might have led to
words of courtship and the future. Now this little window
into how Sam saw her gave Erica a moment of unmatchable
joy. She didn't care a farthing that Sam's own literacy
seemed to be spent on one author, and possibly one book.

They set off brash and larky for the wedding. They were
rude to be having Erica go at all, and arrived so late that
the meal was finished and the handsome room looked stale
and disrespected by rumpled linens, dirty glasses, nobody
sitting still in his proper place. Erica at once drew in her
skirts, despised the bride and groom, the wedding guests, as
if they were people who ought to have cleaned up after
themselves. They found Sam's mother, who just looked cross
and pink-faced like any reasonably impatient mother, and
Sam said, "This is Lady Brett, Mother," and Erica said, "How
do you do, Mrs. Ives?" in impeccable American, and Mrs.
Ives shook her hand but said to Sam, "Look at the time, Sam!
Your behavior is simply inexcusable." He kissed her cheek
and asked, "Where's Dad?" but Dad had had one of his
bilious attacks and had taken a cab home earlier.

Sam introduced Erica as Lady Brett to a lot of people who
wouldn't have caught the name whatever it was, it being too
late in the party, so it wasn't much of a literacy test. The
bride was blond and rather strapping, a head-swiveler whose
eyes were always searching out the next but one. "Sam dar-

ling, I've got to escape! Will they ever let me sneak out of here!" she said quite loudly. A man who looked a lot like her joined her left arm. "You haven't met my husband," she said to Erica. "This is Lady Brett," Sam said to the groom, and the groom said mechanically, "Awfully nice of you to come."

"I've got to get some air, I've got to get out of here," Erica whispered to Sam, and when they were out on Park again she said, "I don't know what's the matter with me! I was swept by the most curious wave of embarrassment for her . . . Geraldine. I suddenly thought, it's indecent to be looking at her. Do you know why? Oh no, no not . . . oh, Sam. What I mean is that a wedding is a celebration of such *failure* for a woman . . . a failure to take hold of life . . . a great *quitting* ceremony. Do you know what I mean? I mean, it made me blush to think there I was staring at her in a moment of her most awful humiliation."

"I don't think old Geraldine really knew how bad the situation was, dearie," he said, smiling beautifully at her, and he took her hand tightly and he walked west toward Fifth while she flew. And the next day, when they dropped in on an old flame of his, now married, a really very nice person, Erica nonetheless had another shudder of revulsion against settling down and having the piano tuned and looking through fabric samples from the decorator's books. And when they had left that apartment and were out on the street Erica's soul soared at the sight of Sam's shocking good looks and she said, "Oh Sam, how I love you! How I love being free."

"Love?" Sam asked quietly, and with his voice he clipped her wings. "Well, I guess it was bound to come up in the course of time. I guess I'm in love with you." He sounded helpless. He sounded as though he had lost a struggle, and one is never absolutely happy about losing a struggle. As declarations go, this one was not too satisfying. They put it behind them, and when he brought her home late that night and they slipped into the living room and fumbled on the couch, Sam didn't say it was love, and Erica was unnerved by the worry of being caught, of Ellen's wandering out in her bathrobe and asking "Sam who?"

On Sunday after breakfast Erica was about to bolt when her grandfather said, "Come on inside with me, Ric, will you? I think it's time we had a little talk about what you're going to do next year." She followed him and sat on the edge of her chair opposite his leather chair, and said sheepishly and untruthfully, "Well, I suppose I'll do shorthand and typing at the Y on 53rd Street." He blinked and settled an afghan around his shoulders where his pain was, and he said, "You know, Ric, that I am not a religious man. But I have a reverence for life. There's something Darwin writes that I'd like to show you. It's in *The Origin of Species,* if you'll just . . . on the top left in the Harvard Classics. I think it's Volume 11."

Erica brought him the brown book and stood by his chair and said hesitantly, "Grandpa, I can't stay this time very long because I've got to . . ."

"Sit down." She sat down. "Here it is: 'When I view all beings not as special creations, but as the lineal descendants of some few beings which lived long before the first bed of the Cambrian system was deposited, they seem to me to become ennobled.' "

He looked at her thoughtfully and she looked at him thoughtfully and he said, "Now I'm going to read it again: 'When I view all beings . . .' " and Erica, who could not focus on it the first time, could not the second either.

"What I want to say is," he explained, "that the understanding that man and his civilization are not special creations but are the consequence of an infinitely marvelous interaction of energy and chance—that fact seems to me more remarkable, more humbling, than if we were here by divine plan. To me it is more ennobling and not less that Aristotle, Shakespeare, Darwin, Wilson, Brandeis, Holmes did not owe their larger vision to the caprice of an omniscient power." He paused.

"Now to the extent that I understand this," he continued, "it entails an *obligation* from me . . . to honor life by living it as richly and responsibly as it is in my compass to do. And I believe you think so too, Ric. I know you accept this obligation, in Justice Holmes' words, 'to share the passion and action of your time at peril of being judged not to have lived.' "

Erica sat quiet, feeling defensive and oppressed by the moral authority of her grandfather, her attention constantly ricocheting between his words and the tugging Sam.

"Now the only way to honor life is to grow through it," he went on. "And the growth of the self is the growth of the mind. I don't have to tell you that. It is a perpetual building upon what one is, an enlarging. That is character. Now character has a *theme*, a blend of purpose and taste, that runs right through a life span . . . like a spine through the body." Pause. "You can't afford to lose sight of the long thrust of your life. You know that, but I'm reminding you." He stopped, allotting her fair time for rebuttal.

"Well, I know I've disappointed you," she said, "and I don't want to hurt you because I think you are the finest man alive, but I've become repelled by the law. It seems to me the least noble profession of them all, altogether cut off from its roots, from justice, from the defense of the rights of man. The terrible witch-hunting, the Un-American Activities Committee, people riding roughshod over anybody with an independent thought—the intimidation—and it's all as if it were no business of the law . . . nothing to do with lawyers and courts. It reminds me so exactly of *Bleak House*. We're right out of Dickens. The men in Ryan's class are absolutely not upset about any of it . . ."

"But not Ryan."

"Oh well, Ryan! Ryan thrives on being contrary."

"It doesn't have to be the law. You're quite right to with-draw now—to reconsider—if you have these doubts. Some-times I think it doesn't matter what discipline you choose as long as you make it your own. Each one, after all, is the his-tory of the growth of man's understanding of his world taken from a particular vantage point. It doesn't make a great deal of difference whether it is philosophy, the law, poetry . . ."

He let her loose. She rebounded to Sam, for whom the future was a contemptible concept, a bogey for the small man who is whipped and checked by fear of what will come next, and Sam was not a small man. The only next for him was a day away, sometimes a minute. Still, there were things he wanted to do.

"Too bad you're no yachtsman," he said to her. "There's something I'm dying to try. Actually, you'd do all right for a canal barge." What he wanted to do was steer a boat through the canals of central France that he had followed by jeep at the end of the war. He could not get over those ca-nals, how straight they were cut along the edge of meadow-land, how straight were the lines of poplars on either side, how frequent were the locks, and steep, how the cabins of the barges had geraniums by the wheel and diapers drying on their decks. "One thing that's always kept me hesitating was boredom." Sam, it had long since been established, was especially sensitive to boredom and was alert to its many disguises. "It's a long slow cruise. After the first twenty locks, you know . . . but you'd keep me amused."

"I can't get over how handsome you are."

"For Chrissake, weren't you listening to me being pas-toral?"

"I was waiting for the part where I'm beautiful."

"The only thing is where would we get the money? I'm stony . . . I've got eight dollars and seventy-three cents un-til July first."

"Well, we'll have to move into my money. I've got plenty

of money," she said, drifting along the canals of his day-dream, thinking about red geraniums and France, where she'd never been.

Three days before her graduation Sam and Erica had a farewell feast with her money at the hotel in Northampton. Vicissitudes of obligation would keep them separated for two weeks. Two weeks cut off from this tumbling passionate indifference to the old business of daily life, two weeks was too frighteningly long for Erica. Sam drifted, Sam wandered. He could not be tied down and be purposeful and do the right things like sleep at night or go to medical school or go to work—not counting a summer job at the Yacht Club—talk about trivial . . . but he was absolutely busted. The last thing she wanted to do, God knows, was tether him, force him to submit to a nine-to-five life. Why, didn't she revel in the very looseness of his being? Why, hadn't he sprung her spirit? Set her free? By loving him she had been able to sweep away countless petty rules and injunctions that had cluttered her life and now in a great white heat from a cold white wine she swept away the big rule, the big injunction. Intolerable to wait two weeks and, not tolerating it, she was over the hurdle and upstairs in Sam's dark pokey room in the grip of an excitement that was not actually sexual. It was a contest with herself but Billie was in it. She was matched against Billie not for Sam but for guts. She was beating.

In the black room she couldn't see Sam ripping off his clothes, couldn't see, thank God, what it looked like; but he was light-years away, not making love the two of them to-gether, but single-mindedly after his own release. He didn't say a word, only breathed heavily and left her on her own to undress and got her on the bed and was graceless and rough with her, and she lay boldly naked, naked to the parts of her body which she would not even name. Sam, in grim dis-regard of her response, bore into her, came in a second and collapsed in relief on top of her, whoever she was. That was

the deflowering, the coming of age in America. She would
have liked to say, "There, there, it doesn't matter. I'm satisfied in my way." He slid from her hips and curled away from
her, and was he dozing?

She lay in a kind of triumph. It was not untinged by the
disappointment that her passion had so abruptly dissolved.
Were the vulgarity of a car and the furtiveness indispensable
to her excitement? Good God. Yes, good God and good daemon, she thought, and smiled into the dark. They said you
would feel absolutely rotten the next morning but she
wouldn't. "I'm regretless," she said to herself.

Sam rolled back to her, rumpled her hair, and asked "You
all right?" in what was to be his one direct reference to the
culmination of their passion. Oh, she was great, she said earnestly. "I don't want you to worry for a minute," he said, re-
ferring to the consequences of that culmination. "You know,
you're almost sure to be safe the first time. It almost never
happens the first time. Really never." She wasn't worried
about anything, she said. She was just happy, she said, and
was more than willing to stay the night, but Sam hadn't
lost his mind, he said, with graduation Sunday, and he got
them dressed and back to the door just under the nose in an
uncharacteristic burst of purpose. And all that was left to
wonder was whether the daemon had a sentimental regard
for the furrow he had plowed.

Chapter 8

Now Erica knew everything, all the large things—"things insolent or things unwonted, things beyond and outside her moira"—and it puffed her up marvelously. And there was an echo: "If I ever have a daughter," Billie had said, "I'm going to name her Moira."

From on top of the world, next afternoon, she watched with superb patience as Mr. Caplan's pre-war station wagon, not the white convertible, crept through the quad. She slipped like Alice Through the Looking Glass back to her old child self and brought them all—Mr. Caplan, her mother and grandparents—to their lace-curtained, bay-windowed, antimacassared inn where two rooms were reserved under the name of Phillips, and Mr. Caplan thoughtfully took the one with the double bed; they would have to make do. This, although she marveled how attractive Mr. Caplan was for a man who must be forty or fifty. And Ellen—she had gained weight and seemed softened. For somebody that ought to be past all that she looked like somebody not past all that.

"Where's Frank?" Ellen whispered. "He's thumbing," said Erica, who would be generous about Ryan.

"Have you thought over our last conversation?" her grandfather asked her before tea. Her answer clicked back and forth against the sides of her skull No, No, No, like a billiard ball, and she said Yes.

"Good. Well, I have an offer for you," he said. "A fine way to waste your summer. Your old Aunt Trudy was on the phone again. She tells me she's yielded to Billie's pleading and taken a cottage in Moriches for the season. You know they are all installed in an apartment on Lexington now that the house is sold. Billie says it is her last carefree summer, the swan song of her girlhood."

"Trudy means to have one more crack at that Ives boy," said her grandmother.

"They want you to come out there, Ric, for as long as you like," said her grandfather.

"That kind of person tends to get what he wants because he's undeflected by finer considerations," her grandmother continued.

"What do you know about the Ives boy, Grandma?" Erica asked, with an edge to her voice.

"The Ives boy? I'm talking about your Aunt Trudy."

"Well, I've signed up to work for Wallace in New York this summer," Erica lied. "I like my adulthood. I don't feel sentimental about the passing of my girlhood and I don't have the time to weep for the passing of Billie's girlhood. What am I to Moriches and Moriches to me?"

Her grandfather blinked when people talked nonsense. He blinked a lot more lately than he used to. His lifetime supply of patience was running out. His face was often drawn with displeasure and, it may be, pain. Erica would address her attention to this pain of his when she had a moment. In the hallway Ellen's voice said, "There you are, Frank! How nice to see you again." They all knew she was finished with Ryan and they would close ranks to protect him, that was clear. Well, fine.

Old cocksure Ryan, what a professional poor boy . . . and those Mongolian cheekbones . . . and he was too thin to be a grown man . . . with a brand-new summer jacket, seersucker, and my God it was probably the first one he ever had that covered his wristbones.

He delivered a large heavy gift into her arms. "Here you are, my proud duchess," the note said, "in remembrance of a worshipful commoner. Ryan."

"I thought," said the commoner, "that now you've come of age the lord only knows where you'll sail off to . . . and I brought you some ballast."

She unwrapped the party paper and it was the Webster's Unabridged Dictionary, and how he could have scratched the money together! "Oh Ryan," she said, overcome by the weight of it. How nice of him, how nice of him, and how he always managed to ground her!

"For those times when you feel you lack definition," he said.

"Frank," said her grandmother with great warmth, "nobody could have thought of a nicer present." Since he was safely spurned by her granddaughter she had forgiven him completely for living in a Boston tenement with his father the fireman and his mother who laundered the altar cloths of St. Polycarp's Church and his seven brothers and sisters.

Erica presided at tea and the lace curtains billowed at the open windows like nun's veiling in the sea wind and all that remained was for Ryan to know that he was spurned, that she was free and safe. It had been understood that each of them was free. Nonetheless, she had felt herself at the end of a long tether. Oh red-cheeked boy fresh from the barber's, with your black hair combed slick, how to get it across to you? Theirs was a sort of platonic relationship about which they were smug. It was superior to other kinds, and it was difficult to see where the claims were made, she upon him, he upon her.

And they were always quarreling about politics or something, always in a tug of war. Why, she had wondered countless times, would she not pull away altogether? "Erica tells us you've got a job as a hospital orderly this summer," said Ellen to Ryan. "I bet she didn't tell you I was working nights for the re-election of Truman," said Ryan to Ellen, with his usual intention to provoke Erica.

"God, Ryan, you're such a trimmer," said Erica, not at all provoked. However, it was evenly divided among the six of them sitting in the circle of this parlor as to who should be president. Mr. Caplan (now called Simon) and her mother were with Erica for Henry Wallace, but both her grandparents were steady on with Truman. Erica had to disallow their being trimmers. Only Ryan, she thought, and what kind of fateful dialectical tensions kept her connected to him?

It wasn't sex. At times when they found themselves drawn toward a physical intimacy Frank checked himself from a sense of propriety he seemed to reserve toward her. His sexual restraint was not disagreeable and was in fact mildly intriguing. She dimly understood it to mean that there were mores where he came from that took care of that sort of thing, mores with girls. Or, alternatively, as his whole program for getting out of the tenement was based upon present denial, this sort of thing was the sort of thing deferred. It left her unspoken for. But it was all the more difficult to call off what had never been called on.

"My grandfather has offered to foot a trip to Europe," she opened to Ryan when he was walking her to her door that night, her last night at Smith, "and I think I'll take him up on it . . . in September. I've changed a lot, Ryan. I guess I need . . ."

"*I've* changed a lot," he said, moving in with two elbows,

typically. "Ever since I've known you, Thoroughgood, I've been fighting against your moral arrogance but, Mother of God, it's all up with me. I've caved in. I'm here to tell you that I've renounced hypocrisy, forsworn it once and for all. I've backslid right out of the church. It's another graduation present for you and it cost me more than the damn dictionary. It cost me my political future."

"Oh Ryan, my God, I don't want you to leave the church on my account!"

"For crying out loud! You know me better than that. I didn't leave it on *your account*. It's a trick of fate, your turning up, that's all."

"If you've left the Catholic Church for Fate then you've just regressed. I hate Fate," she snapped. Ryan ignored her and pursued his own train of thought.

"My people are decent people," he said, almost musing. "I don't have to be ashamed of them. I know my old man hits the bottle once in a while but it's our cultural phenomenon. At least he doesn't hit my mother, which is also a cultural phenomenon. They're decent people . . . it's not that. . . . But do you remember that afternoon you and I went up to the Cloisters with your mother and Mr. Caplan? We got out of the subway into a wet snow squall and we went trudging up the hill and it was stony cold outside and in. Well, I was walking with your mother, looking at those madonnas and crucifixions and altar pieces and I thought, sweet weeping Jesus—that may be primitive art to them but it's primitive religion to me and it scares the hell out of me. Then when we were standing in front of something, I forget, your mother said, 'Every once in a great while,' she said, 'I see a painting or a piece of sculpture and I transcend my own limitations. And I'm exalted. You would think, Frank,' she said, 'that working in the field as I do it would be a common experience. But I'm talking about a height I don't often reach,' she said, 'I'm brushed by an angel's wing . . . and

I'm humbled that it has ever happened to me at all. Whatever I am,' she said, 'I'm not so small as I would have been if I'd never touched that height.' " Ryan was quiet for a moment and then he went on, "I say my people are decent, but knowing you, your mother, your grandfather, the whole lot, Ric, I've not only come to understand a wider decency than I've ever known, really, but I've got to live by it. I'm not so small as I would have been, that's all I mean."

Erica listened and was stirred but she had no way to take all this Ryanism in. If you've made somebody a better man it puts a lien on you. But there wasn't space for any more liens on Erica's emotion. She murmured that he wasn't ever small and left him with whatever assumptions he had about her undebated.

She left everybody to their assumptions. A crescendo of love, of pride in her, was building in all her people, suitably, because she was to receive high honors at her commencement. Next morning she received them with grace, or at least nobody criticized her performance until they were on their way back to New York, the car packed to the rafters. "I don't know why that boy puts up with you," her grandfather said irritably out of the clear blue sky. Nobody answered him since probably nobody knew why either. Erica stayed quiet. She was not ambitious to do a great deal more than keep her family at bay.

Once home again she hardly heard her family, hardly saw them, and only wondered occasionally that they weren't agog at the amazing metamorphosis of their own proper thoroughgood child. She had become a gypsy. She had become a star. Through the following twelve days of empty time and space she was mad-dash bohemian who wore gold bangle earrings and a black linen suit through a week-long sweltering hot spell while her grandmother said a hundred times how black takes on the heat, dear. Her imagination was as busy as ten nimble fingers at designing and redesigning patterns for the next spate of time in which she and Sam might be on a little canal boat or in a little village in Burgundy or a little apartment in Paris, though she could not recall Sam's face, could not reconstruct it for the scenes he had to play. That was a perverse silly trick of the mind.

His camera clicking every minute and she never had a snapshot of him, and by their rules there were no phone calls, no letters, to resubstantiate him. It was easier with France, which she saw through Impressionist eyes, through Bonnard in particular, but also through the travel folders at Cook's, from whom she inquired, interesting but bored in her black suit, about steamship passage to Cherbourg for September. The settings for her life with Sam were rich in detail but the plot tended to flag. She would assign Sam a purpose, like writing a book at their flat on the Left Bank, but it lacked verisimilitude. For herself she provided the tender ministering role, quiescent, satisfied, and not very likely either. She made omelets with herbs or watered the geraniums or wore a suit of bottle-green velvet, but on a barge? It was unreasonable to let her mind devise some intellectual adventure for itself. After all, there was no joy from a fantasy that would catapult a headlong mad-dash bohemian beauty out of a passionate romance as fast as it had flung her in. When the plot problem arose about life in the intervals of passion she would scratch that script, begin on another. But always in France. The very Frenchness of her scenes revived her nostalgic though feeble tie with her drowned father, who had courted her mother in Paris, where she had very nearly been born.

Meanwhile day followed night like night the day and finally Erica almost wearily was able to return to earth to meet the Sunday-evening express from Montauk. Penn Station was crowded with people coming back from their weekends, and there were no taxis for them and too few redcaps and it was like an oven with the smell of locomotives cooking in it. Erica was damp with excitement or from the black suit and scanned with brisk efficiency every one of the million faces that she met and could not understand how she'd missed Sam's. She knew for a certainty that he had not come off the 8:15 while not believing it, and shot upstairs and down and checked every impossibility while a nausea swelled her throat and sound roared in her ears and finally, breaking all their rules, she dialed the Ives home number in New York and had let it ring at least six times when Sam's voice said a dull hello.

"Sam! What are you doing there?" Erica said in a voice pitched high.

"Oh hell, I slept right through, didn't I?" Sam said, only mildly abashed.

"But why aren't you on the 8:15?"

"Well, the fact of the matter is, dearie, I got fired from the club for insubordination or sleeping in the noonday sun. You know, I should never take a job that starts in the morning. They had me up there sitting on my wooden pillar every day, Saint Sam the Stylite, watching for people to drown, and clunk! my eyes'd shut, and I'd go out like a light. They had to drown without my watching and their feelings got hurt. People are oversensitive about . . ."

"Sam, are you going to come and get me?" It was a cry of anguish although it might have sounded like an order.

"Let's see now," Sam said with deliberate quiet. "What time is it? After nine—oh boy. I'll tell you what. There's nobody here. You just hop a cab and I'll be downstairs in front of the door to meet you, and that way I can have a wash and be pretty for you."

A wave of revulsion at the choice of his "pretty" rolled against her sudden desperate intention not to be abandoned and she sent out another order in a shrewish voice that covered her with shame: "Say that you love me!"

"Listen, Ric, will you calm down now?" Sam's voice was

gentle and reasonable and grown-up. "All I did was over-sleep. If you wanted somebody wide-awake you should never have taken me on. Listen, I'll tell you what we'll do. Give me twenty minutes and wait for me across the street at the Pennsylvania and," he sang, "I'll be down to get you in a taxi, honey . . ."

"I was just so disappointed not to see you here," she said slowly, feeling herself shrivel, while at the same time trying to undo some fatal thing that she had done. "I haven't thought of anything but you and it's been such a long time and I worried so when you weren't on the train."

"God knows I've been worried about you Ric. You all right?"

"Well, I'll be all right when I just see you . . ."

"I mean . . . you know . . . about that other thing . . ."

"Oh that? That's fine Sam," she said, the shriveling continuing at an even, relentless pace. She tried to stop it and said with good cheer, "You know what I've discovered? You can book third-class passage on the *Queen Mary* sailing September seventh for a hundred and ninety-five dollars a person."

"Third class! That's steerage! That's for the peasants and their ducks. We'll talk about it. A lot of things have come up. Now listen, Erica, you do what I say. Go on over to the Pennsylvania. You can get a cup of coffee while you're waiting, and then I'll be down to get you in a taxi, honey." It was too much for Erica.

"I won't be there," she said as if with her last breath, and hung up.

Chapter 9

For those last three months of her girlhood Erica had been a proud beauty. At least she had known that. Wonderfully indifferent to the hootings of the flat-earthers, she had sailed straight out across the unknown sea like a little flagship breasting the winds, a brazen and regal *Santa Maria*. As it turned out, the earth was flat and she fell over the edge. In Sam's voice on the telephone she heard the pending jilt and in the nick of time was able to save at least her face. She was not shocked that he would leave her, but only shocked by how soon. All along she had half, or better one quarter, known his reluctance to bother venturing himself in a life of heroic proportion. He was not suited for a proper daemon. He was too soft, and a kind of coward. When she got home from the station she called him again and was weeping while he did not answer the phone. If he had answered, what humiliation she might have piled upon herself she would not later guess. Would she have sobbed without control, accused him of weakness and breaches of faith, and calculated his immense debt to her with the head for figures of a woman spurned? And however could he pay it? The only way he could pay it was by finding harpies irresistible. Sam spared her all this by seeing the immediate advantage of being set free to the alternative of a prolonged wriggling out. Probably he had left town, she thought.

The summer set in and the three quarters of her ached from a broken heart and one quarter felt fascinating because of it. She might easily pass for twenty-five and her self-esteem hung on the thought. Otherwise her self-esteem was in the poorest condition. She had never before seen herself, her judgment, her intentions as matters of indifference to the world. Even her family all at once stopped finding her of central significance. She was suffering and she hid her suffering from them and they didn't notice. If it hadn't been Sam, if it hadn't been the Ives boy, she might have told her whole long story in her mother's arms. Her grandfather, whose temper was short these days, snapped, "What's the matter with you?" and she might have blurted out what was, but something was the matter with him. Her grandmother said that Mrs. Goodman, who lived in a neighboring apartment, was looking for a baby-sitter for the afternoons. "A baby-sitter, Grandma! Goodness!"

"Well, you aren't doing anything. If you let yourself drift pointlessly you will become demoralized." Her grandmother spoke sternly and knitted with her arthritic fingers. Good old Simon Caplan knew somebody and stopped her drift. He pointed her toward Altman's, where she became a summer salesgirl in Better Sportswear. She sold camel's hair coats and plaid kilts and when a customer looked down upon her wares she would have liked to suggest Worser Sportswear. Often she forgot she was grieving.

It was a rehearsal of grief, a mock grief, a foretaste of the true thing. One afternoon after about four weeks of patronizing her customers she came home to find her whole family sitting in the living room watching for her. Immediately she went to her grandfather, dropped to her knees, reached her hands awkwardly around his chest, and asked, "What is it?"

"Cancer of the lung."

"How can that be?" she protested, "how can that be? The pain was in your neck!"

He looked at her mildly, patted her arm, and didn't say anything.

"Oh, I can't live without you, I can't bear to lose you, I can't," she whispered through her tears.

"Yes you can," he said, calmly patting.

"How much time do they let you have?"

"They let me have a little time . . . enough."

"Oh, I love you so," she sobbed as quietly as she could manage, and she was for the moment reassured by her fingers that felt him still perfectly alive beneath the familiar smooth cotton of his white shirt. That his life would soon slip through them was unacceptable.

But acceptance came and there was to be no moaning at the bar. They all had a Tom Collins and then they all had another and it was like the Declaration of War followed by the war effort, a portentous unencompassable event followed by existence uncannily like what one always knew. Her grandfather went off to his office in the mornings, but came home at noon to rest. While his spirits were so fine the days were like half holidays, pleasant, almost festive. He took pills, had no appetite, and began rereading *War and Peace*. "I am like Napoleon at Moscow. My luck has run out," he said, but not regretfully. Erica wondered how he could choose such a long book. For about three weeks it was as though after they'd announced a disaster they'd called it off.

"Aren't we abnormal to be so everyday? Grandpa seems actually cheerful. I can't understand it," she said to Ellen.

"He has no pain. They've put him on something very strong. And of course he's suspected for some time that this was going to be a bad story, so that he's rid of the uncertainty at least. It's a relief to know, curiously."

"A relief! I don't see how in your wildest dreams you can call such a thing a relief!"

"Haven't you ever known that something you hoped for was destined to have an ending you didn't want so that finally when it happened you were upset, of course, but you also were set free?"

"Ach! How can you say that about dying? He's going to lose us all," Erica said irritably.

"Well, and of course he's not going to miss you!" Ellen snapped. Her mother could sound just like her grandfather when he'd had enough.

Then one August day became the last time he would go to his office. The starch went out of him abruptly and he only wanted to be in his bed and couldn't be lured out of it. He was in no way stalwart any more. He slept, complained, withered. Before their eyes this large man curled smaller beneath the bedsheets. Down he went through the whole month of September, but not out. A nurse was installed and an oxygen tank in a corner, not used yet but a sign of inexorability. Wilson flew in from California. He seemed numbed. All their nerves became taut from the interminable dying and each one of them disguised his exasperation with the inhumanity of nature. It silenced them. They had less and less they were willing to say. Erica's grandmother hobbled in and out of her husband's room, her large old jutting jaw designed for disapproval. Ellen managed them all and was the calmest, having Simon Caplan to catch her if she fell. Simon had to catch Wilson, prop him up. Wilson was the only one of them who could not stand this death. Never close to his father, nor satisfactory to him, he could not now somehow use the time of the slow dying to accustom himself to the death. The others used the time. Erica too.

And then unexpectedly her grandfather came back to life

again. His mind cleared. He resumed *War and Peace*. Emaciated though he looked, his voice was strong and he liked a conversation. One October evening at rest on this peaceful plateau he motioned for Erica to sit by him and said, "No part of life is uninteresting and dying isn't either, up to a point. . . . Pain—after a while pain is boring, overwhelmingly boring. When I'm free of it as I am now, its absence is a positive pleasure. My first pure experience with the theory of utility. Of course, if you have to wait to die for it then it isn't terribly useful."

"You're making this into a tract for me," Erica said, smiling, amazed that his mind had recaptured all its lost territory. "You're a Jusquaboutist, precept and example all the way to the end."

"Jusquaboutist? That's very good. Where did you get it?"

"From browsing in my new dictionary."

"Ah! That's what I wanted to tell you. I knew there was something. At the end of the summer when I was putting my affairs in order I wrote to Frank asking him to come to see me."

"Ryan?" She was startled. "Because of the law, I hope, and not because of me."

"Because of the law. Although you might do a great deal worse than Frank, Erica. I wanted to introduce him to members of the firm. As you know, he and I have discussed the possibility of our finding a place for him."

"And he didn't come?"

"Oh yes, he came. We had a long talk about his future. He's at sixes and sevens too. He thinks of teaching. I asked him to stay the night but he had bought a round-trip excursion-rate ticket."

And he had made no effort to see her. How easy everybody found it to scuttle off. What a sinking ship she must look.

"He's a man of pride, Erica," her grandfather added in mild rebuke.

In a day or two he resumed dying and finished conveniently on Halloween night. He joined the saints while they were up and about. The following Sunday there was a memorial service and the chapel was filled. Billie and her mother were there. Notwithstanding the great numbers coming and going and finding their seats, Erica saw them again and again and Billie's eye would not let her go. Afterward a fat and furry winter Aunt Trudy, her powered face wet with tears, and looking like a tragic soprano about to sing some of her sobs, hugged Erica and kissed her on two cheeks and said, "My poor, poor child. I pity you with all my heart, You are too young to appreciate your loss. You'll never know what a man he was. Incomparable! Peerless! I know. I flatter myself I was among those precious few who understood his worth. When you are older, Erica, you will live to regret . . ."

"Mummeeee!" moaned Billie, who was stronger than her mother and bumped her to the side. Then she put her arms around Erica, burst into tears herself, and said, "I'm heartbroken for you. I know he was everything to you. There are so many things to cry over. I've got to see you. You're the person in the world I love best."

Standing straight as a lean good child in her black dress, Erica was truly bereft, down to the bone, and returned the love freely to this helplessly beautiful half-sister with her beaver coat not even pulled on straight. The next afternoon she left her shorthand school, where she had not made a single friend, not one, and feeling all waif, shivered in a thin raincoat down dark grey 53rd Street to meet Billie at Pierre's. Billie was late. Erica, her chin up for the challenge and looking more like her grandmother than she would have liked to know, defied any waiter in the nearly empty restaurant to throw her out for not seeming suitable. Cowed, they led her to a table where she waited, propping her chin elegantly, sister to all pensive blooming women who sat at white-clothed tables for Renoir, Manet, Lautrec to paint. But her confidence had forsaken her. She shifted her elbow, dropped her chin, and considered the absinthe drinkers, who were gaunt and suffered.

Billie came and suited Pierre's wonderfully, and instead of absinthe ordered Brandy Alexanders because Erica needed to put on weight. Billie said that her own gluttony was at war with her vanity over the terrain of her stomach. She needed to keep her stomach flat to set off her handsome hipbones and she was in the habit of putting her finger down her throat after a big meal, did Erica ever? Erica shook her head, smiling and humble before such disgusting courage, and murmured, "Oh, Billie."

Billie said with great affection, "You don't have the inclination to be bad. Solid as a rock. You know who you are, where you're going. I am, on the other hand, in an agony of uncertainty . . . division . . . deceit . . ."

"For crying out loud, Billie, I'm every bit as uncertain and divided and deceitful as you," said good and guilty Erica. "You give yourself airs!"

"I'm in a miserable mess, Ric. I need to talk to you," Billie went on, and her eyes filled with tears. "There isn't another person I know I'd want to confide anything in. And my mother . . . I'm not a bit like you. I'm heading right for disaster. And the thing is, any girl I know would give her eyeteeth to head for it instead. It's crazy. . . . Listen, Ric. I have a proposal. What's the possibility of our getting an apartment together? I mean it. I can't swing one myself. I've absolutely got to get away from my mother. The miserable irony of it is that all my life I've headed for New York and just when I'm home free she's gotten there first!

"And I can't find a decent job . . . a degree from Vassar isn't worth two cents. You know that. And I refuse to do what you're doing because I will not be admirable. Anyway, there isn't any job I could get that I want.

"I'm not fooling about the apartment, Ric. If you can't

come to my rescue I'll have to marry Sam. Do you remember Sam? I'm quite desperate."

Erica, flushed out of her silence, said, "I thought you were through with him?"

"Everybody's changed the rules. Instead of being free-wheeling and having a good time they've begun to pair off like frightened rabbits. It's revolting. I have nothing but contempt for them. And for myself. What do you think of me?"

"Well, I just thought it was all over," Erica repeated, very rocked.

"The joke was on me," Billie said. Two tears formed in the corners of her eyes and she blotted them with the damp cocktail napkin. "You know, we finally went to Moriches last summer. We took that lovely cottage on the bay that's next to the mother house. Do you remember? Where the nuns used to walk up to the lilac hedge? Well, on the other side. I borrowed a car and brought Mummy and Uncle Tony out. Effie had gone ahead on the train. It was a beautiful June day, windy, big white clouds, the water choppy, and I think I was never so happy in my life. I felt finally free. I'd acquitted myself, got my degree, and now the world was mine, and about time. I drove right on up to the Yacht Club in Westhampton Beach absolutely filled with self-confidence. And the very first guy I see is Sam. He was a life guard and he looked terrific, and I thought all I need to do is whistle and he'll come running. The idea made me sick, absolutely sick. So I said to myself, 'Okay, Billie, don't get your kidneys in an uproar. Don't whistle! That's all.' Oh God, God, God, I feel the brandy," she said in her hushed husky way, and put the heels of her hands into her eyes.

Erica felt the brandy and asked, "When did you whistle?"

"Well, I want to tell you something. I wasn't on that beach an hour when it was clear as day I was going to be left on that beach high and dry if I didn't watch my step. *Everybody* was engaged or going steady and everybody was in the biggest goddam hurry to tell me that Sam had somebody."

"Who?"

"I haven't an idea. Nobody in the gang. I don't even think it was true. But I panicked. I really panicked. I'm really crazy about it out there . . . Moriches, the ocean at West-hampton Beach . . . I love sailing, tennis . . . I don't have the guts to give it up. If I had *real* money . . . and where would I go?"

"What have you said to Sam?"

"Oh, he's in Edinburgh. Do you remember I told you he was going to medical school in Edinburgh? So I really have this winter to see if I can get out of this bind."

PART THREE
1970

⚘

Chapter 10

Erica walked diagonally across the great trapezoid of lawn to its narrowest angle by the creek mouth where an old butternut tree grew as large as life. She had not remembered there having been a tree there at all. She thought there had been a widow's walk but the roof of the mother house was gabled, and as she turned for a moment to see it again the shingles looked a dark black-green as if they were covered by lichen. It was an illusion cast by the shadow of heavy branches.

The butternut by the creek mouth was one of life's unexpected gifts. She had bought three white wicker chairs to try under it and admired the look of them now with her brother-in-law Robbie, another unexpected gift, sitting in one and her visiting mother and Simon in the other two. Propped against the mottled yellow bark was her oblivious younger daughter Honora, who was fifteen and reading while chewing love-knots into her dark brown hair. It was a breezy June morning. Countless small boats dotted the dark water. The flat land bloomed a young green to the very edge of the great bay. The bay was polluted to the gills.

"We were thinking," said Ellen in greeting, "how after all these years you are finally back in your beloved Moriches. We were thinking as we slapped our mosquitoes that your cup must be full. Well, your cup is always full," she added a little unctuously. Ellen and Erica had an affectionate and companionable rapport but they had managed their womanhood very differently. Ellen thought she had been a splendid model of independence for her daughter, upon whom it had been utterly wasted. Erica was altogether domesticated, round and contented. On her side, Erica was a little defensive about being so wholesome and fretted at her mother's sometimes-labored praise. She suspected Ellen found it handy to endow her with such an oversupply of domestic virtue so that she might herself draw on the surplus, as for instance finding a daughter so married as to obviate the need of a mother's having to marry at all.

"You know," Erica said, "from the house you look beautiful, all of you, sitting under the tree. Out of Chekhov, the first act."

"Because of being esthetic and decadent," Simon acquiesced. "Your mother is very keen on being decadent," he added in a fond way, and got up to give Erica his seat. Erica protested but he said he needed to move about as he was getting stiff in his old age. Ellen had gotten fat in hers.

"I have some news," said Erica. "Who do you think takes the cottage on the other side of the lilacs? Aunt Trudy! Can you believe the coincidence?" Well, they couldn't. They talked about Trudy and about Billie's not being far behind. It was not strictly speaking a coincidence for Erica, however, since she knew that her Aunt Trudy had once rented that cottage years before but in imagining what she could have been doing for the last twenty summers never thought to keep her coming back to it. Erica heard she would be down for the season the next day, and then things would move quickly. She hadn't thought it would be so quick.

Honora, absorbed in her book, let out a grunt and Robbie said, "We're both reading *Jane Eyre*. She beating." He brushed back his hair from his forehead in order to think, in a characteristic gesture he shared with Frank. They both had the same long lank hair, Robbie's still almost red, Frank's almost black. Honora could think with her hair hanging straight over her eyes, and even read.

"How do you like your book?" Ellen asked her granddaughter.

"Fantastic!" Honora was in the tenth grade of North Bronx Country Day, where the favorite things were Bible Literature and Shoplifting. Both Erica's girls read at a tremendous clip.

"The older I get the more slowly I read," Erica said, supporting the losing Robbie.

The others wandered off and she was alone with Robbie. He was a conundrum to which only a conjectural answer could be made, a bookseller and storyteller, a single man with a large head above an overlarge stomach, but having long elegant legs. She was thinking how none of that fat went to his buttocks or his legs and what about gravity? From the rear he looked like an Edwardian diplomat but from the front one couldn't place him.

"What are you thinking?" he asked Erica.

"I was thinking it was odd they would give red hair to a black sheep. For disguise, I suppose." Robbie was the oldest of the eight children, seven years Frank's senior. She had a sigh for the poor old Ryans. They had worked so hard over each one of their kids, scrubbed the nits out of their hair with yellow soap, starched the white middy blouses, examined their workbooks for gold stars, heard their catechism, kept them on the straight path to a high school diploma. Then with a little paternal push and godspeed from Mama the first thing every one of them did was take a sharp left. But Robbie was their black sheep. He was to be the priest. They believed he instructed the whole flock in the art of straying. Erica had met him for the first time at her own wedding, the only one of Frank's family to turn up, and he stood by, best man before the judge, his bemused, already lined face giving her reassurance and self-doubt in equal measure.

"At the moment *you* look like a Girl Scout leader," he said, "in your white blouse and your tidy blue skirt. However, some Girl Scout leaders look very sensuous to me."

She ignored him and went on to his question. "Really, I was thinking that I am sentimentalized hopelessly by other people, my mother, for instance, and sometimes it gets me down. It makes me feel shallow. Well . . . I think there is something shallow about me."

"Nonsense. You're the most fanatical mind-improver I know."

She might have said the same of him but there was something else on her mind. "Here I am looking across the very grass over which my white nuns used to flutter and now it's all ours. To have been able to buy the mother house and to come back with my own family to the place above all that I loved as a child . . . well, I just seem to have been awfully lucky in my life . . . and now to close the circle . . . I think of it as closing a circle . . . like seeing Billie again after twenty years."

"Oh well, it isn't only luck, Ric. You deserve it. It's just virtue being rewarded."

"That's exactly what makes me uneasy. For nobody else is virtue still being rewarded. Just me. I tell you, it's eerie being the only one for whom the mechanism still works." Erica had for some time been grazing on a field of discontent, or anger, hesitant to take a real mouthful. "Of course," she said, defending herself against attack from herself, "I am lucky to have the knack of being schizophrenic. 'You've got to be schizophrenic,' I've told Lucy quite earnestly. On the one hand you've got to monitor the outside world, read the *Times,* count the bombs, face the implications, and do what must be done as a responsible citizen. Private life is another matter, a preserve where you love and read and the food is good. A lot of one's ho-ho effort goes into keeping the two separate, and of course one can't always. When we went into Cambodia in May, Lucy phoned us from Smith crying her heart out. I couldn't say anything. I was crying too."

"Ah, that's not what's got you down, the encroaching world," said Robbie.

"Down, down," she mused. "You would have to be an idiot not to be down. Frank thinks it's the menopause."

"Frank's a horse's ass."

Erica was long accustomed to bestride the almost physical antipathy the brothers had for each other, two bodies that could not occupy the same place at the same time. She was living her adult life in an untoward situation that she had forced beautifully to be toward, and she was very used to doing so. From the moment the judge had pronounced her wife to the one man, her longing shot off to the other, a story of the switching of infant loves where the wrong one was the prince. This sounded a desperate situation indeed but the actuality was that through pride, through honor, through a delicate sense of responsibility, she espoused a commitment to her choice of husband along with the husband himself. She had fanned her care for Frank. She had tamped her passion for Robbie whether or not it was like tamping clay over a blasting charge. Their attraction for each other remained untalked-about, and in all justice it ought not to have persisted. They ought to have been relieved of it.

Robbie never married. He owned and managed a good bookstore in the Back Bay and dropped in several times a week on his old mother, who still lived in the same slum in the same half of a house with green asbestos shingle clapped on it. Of all the children, Robbie was the only one who reg-

ularly visited the old lady in what he referred to as her semi-
detached villa, and she wasn't grateful. The others thoughtfully sent checks. Besides being a good son, Robbie was an
obsessive traveler. He regarded every mile of dry earth as
something his own feet must walk on, not counting Hawaii
and Australia. He had heard, for instance, that the gurgling
of an elephant's stomach was one of the great sounds of the
universe so he went to Kenya to listen. Through the years
Erica had met two women in whom he had been interested.
Very nice women. He knew by telepathy when Frank would
be out of town, and by telephone.

With some historical perspective, therefore, Erica's marriage might seem to have been less the wedding of two
people, more a consecration of the eternal triangle. It would
have been difficult to attract Frank's attention to the underlying existence of this triangle. Frank was an ambitious hard-
working man who had moved from success to success in the
academic world; a sociable, political, but not, God knows, in-
trospective man was Frank Ryan. For Frank Ryan nothing
could have been more trivial than triangles.

The equilibrium of this aged triangle had not been dis-
turbed by a pinpointable event but it was nonetheless wob-
bling. There was a small shift backward in Robbie's corner.
He had seemed willing to pass his life in a condition of poetic
self-denial, and was anyway reticent and private by nature,
but lately he had become withdrawn, and in the last year or
two when the opportunity to visit Erica occurred he missed
it as often as not. She hadn't seen him for several months and
this gnawed at her. Of course, she told herself, there were
reasons enough to account for his being dispirited, reasons
enough for anybody who read the *Times*. And also his work
had become increasingly unsatisfying. Being proprietor of a
book shop had almost no antiquarian charm left to it; it was
all grim supermerchandizing now. Moreover, Robbie was

fifty-three. Nobody tells a man when to stop and take a reckoning, but he had come of age. Whatever it was, Erica felt some slippage away from her, some ebbing of his pleasure in her, and this situation did not of course buoy her own flagging spirit.

"I longed for you to come down, Robbie. I wanted you to see it all," Erica said as they left the tree and walked along the retaining wall. "You know, I was enormously surprised," she said, "to find that nothing had shrunken, not the houses, not the bay, that my memory had . . . belittled nothing."

"There must be more than a hundred small boats out there," Robbie observed.

"Yes, but they're too late to kill the bay. The old duck farms got there first. There used to be so many crabs when I was little. I used to sneak my net down softly, softly into the water when I spied a crab against the dock post, sea-green and fierce and pretending to nap . . . and I'd *clap* my net to catch him . . . and always miss. Billie never missed. But the crabs are gone because the ducks excrete something they don't like to swim in. They're more fastidious than people."

"The trouble with earlier generations," said Robbie, "is that they killed naïvely, either from rage or, like the duck farmers, by inadvertence. Now we have the technical understanding to see what we are doing without the weakness of allowing our emotions to become too involved. Still, Ric, it's a lovely spot from which to watch the world die."

"It's my place to watch from," she said. "I've watched from here before. When I was a very little girl out there on the beach from the top of my father's shoulders . . . it was a total eclipse . . . and I can still remember my terrible certainty that the world was coming to an end. I was off in my timing."

"Anyhow," Robbie said, looking at her with pained eyes and his crooked affectionate smile, "I love to see you here.

It's a beautiful house and it suits you and you belong here. . . . To come back . . . it can be a tremendously restorative thing to come back to what you love most . . ."

Robbie's eyes were set deep and of a buttery brown color and Erica forced her own eyes away from them. "I don't know what's the matter with me," she said. "Maybe it is premenopausal. Maybe Frank is right. I notice that I don't even read with very much interest, and you know I haven't been able to write at all. It's as if I . . . can't close my own circle. I know my life by today's measure is a bed of roses but . . . it's like the princess and the pea. I sleep on twenty mattresses and all night long I toss and turn and the next morning I have the most terrible bruise on my back . . ."

"You are a true princess, Erica. I never doubted it."

"Ah, but I've lost my way, Rob."

"No, you're right on the mark. Here in Moriches. I'm sure of it. You know that every writer has these fallow times."

Erica was the author of two unknown volumes of essays and a somewhat known writer of popular articles, but she had not been able to write anything for a long time, neither this nor that.

"Muses," she said. "There may be no God but there are certainly muses. . . . I used to have a kind of comfortable supply of *ingenuousness* . . . that I wrote out of, that I lived out of. Well, it's run dry. What I mean is that I realize everybody has to pretend that the little daily things he thinks and does have meaning, are of some consequence, some use. But I've come to the point where I have to pretend to everything from the moment I get up in the morning. . . . I don't *believe* any more. I've lost all that ingenuousness. . . . Well, don't you see, Robbie, that makes me just a pretender. Not a true princess at all."

Chapter 11

As the wife of an academic and mother of two children roosting and clucking for most of her twenty years in a comfortably large fieldstone house at the woodsy edge of the university campus in the North Bronx, Erica had led an exemplary life. Since she was now past forty, with her children grown and her country at the nadir of its moral history, her depression might seem to be exemplary too. And certainly she wasn't the only woman to have trouble suppressing her suppressed resentments. She had quarreled and argued with Frank to the day of her wedding in a not very attractive way, as her grandfather had noted. But her marriage marked the end of her balkiness. It represented a not entirely conscious bargain and she kept her end of it cheerfully, as it was in her nature to do. She swapped baby nuzzling and plant watering and French cooking for the private time in which to read in her own study, and to follow her interest in art through the museums and galleries of the city of New York. This second interest was pleasant but not productive. The first, the reading, the self-teaching, led to her writing. Until this brought her some small recognition she thought she ought to get another degree and teach, which was Frank's good idea. It would have been a good idea if she had had the least inclination for it.

As to bargains, Frank made two felicitous choices in his early life and had no reason to look back. He himself chose teaching instead of the practice of law and he chose Erica instead of anybody else. These choices ratified his inherent confidence in his own superior sense, and it was not his way to let self-doubt hamper him. His very doubtlessness had sent him flying up from the slum, up higher and higher through a full professorship in the School of Law, and then up some more. He had now been dean of the undergraduate School of the Arts and Sciences for four years, a distinguished position, while he continued to teach a course in torts in the law school.

He said he owed everything to Erica, by which he did not, of course, really mean everything.

Erica did in fact make a gracious life for them all and to this day she did not believe it was beneath a woman to spend time doing so. Nonetheless, she was not doubtless as her husband was, and she had begun—with the language of women's liberation shrill in her ears—to entertain the question whether the amorphous self-dissatisfaction, the pointlessness she was now feeling, did not come from a too-willing submission to the classic woman's role. She had trouble defining herself independently of her husband, and even, with some hesitation, tried to talk to him about it, but he said nonsense, he had no trouble defining her at all. To do him justice, he had been in a terrible rush about something, and had gone off glad to have comforted her, but she had had a struggle with a deep erupting anger ever since. In spite of this, she would be the first to say she lived the good life. There were deficiencies in it, of course. There was very little exercise, like skiing or tennis or sex. And she wasn't musical.

When Erica left Robbie to *Jane Eyre* the first thing she did was change from being a Girl Scout leader into a pale blue summer dress with a hairbreadth stripe of white. She had not worn it lately because it was tight and the buttons pulled a little over her breast. It was a gesture that gave her away and she watched herself make it. She might lose five pounds. People thought she was a good-looking woman with a lot of class, and she took pleasure in an elegant appearance. If she had been a real broad, luscious and lust-worthy, accustomed to walking into a roomful of men and hearing all their molecules roll around, she would have taken even more pleasure. But nothing would ever come of the vulgarity in her nature. She gave it too little attention. She wore her hair parted in the middle and held by a clasp at the back of her head. Although she was a princess, there was some grey in it.

Changed now, metamorphosed by a hairbreadth, Erica picked up a paring knife from the kitchen and an armload of fresh asparagus—"brought with me from Fenchurch Street a hundred of Sparrow grass," Pepys had one day noted—and sat on her top porch step to brood. She scaled each sparrow grass with her knife, snapped off its bottom, and took thirty minutes where thirty seconds would have done. She bet her bottom dollar Billie wasn't grey. And what the hell would she look like beside Billie, who was three inches taller and ten times as eye-catching, as she surmised from what Robbie said and also from the woman's page of *The New York Times*. How capriciously were the good things divided between these half-sisters. Erica was left to be the repository of the finer intellectual and moral values. She sighed for it. She was also the repository of a doubt about Robbie and Billie and the spring weeks they once spent together at Stresa. Did they have a love affair? Robbie would never have said. At the time the suspicion had made her quite ill.

Erica had not seen Billie since the winter they were two

girls made distraught by the same Sam. Billie had not stayed distraught long—she hadn't the taste for uncertainty—and married Sam instead. At the time she reminded Erica of Scarlett O'Hara, who saw a lot of disagreeable things piling up but said she would not think about them *today*, and didn't. Billie had phoned to tell Erica about her wedding, and in a voice that carried the very *sound* of a blush had pleaded with her to be her maid of honor. Erica said she was just sick not to be able to, but was leaving that week for Europe, and with an efficiency that was in her nature and an energy generated by shame, discovered a freighter sailing for Rotterdam and was on it that Wednesday at midnight. "I can't understand what's got into you! You have less than a month to go before you earn your secretarial certificate," her grandmother had said as often as the remaining days provided occasion. But her curious mother had said it was good for Erica not to finish something she had started.

Thereafter Erica kept out of Billie's way. It was not hard to do through the years the Iveses were in Edinburgh or afterward when Billie tried to get them together from time to time. Billie was not stick-to-it-ive, God knows. They exchanged letters at Christmas, and Erica was tweaked to watch Billie rack up six children. By keeping her distance, Erica remained free of a mild and barely admitted sexual jealousy not precisely deriving from Sam. More surprising, it wasn't over Robbie either. On the contrary, it was Robbie's clear regard for Billie that dispelled finally the grudging part of her old love for this half-sister.

If that weren't true would she have reversed her policy of steering clear of Billie in order to buy the house in Moriches? Would she have steamed straight into the heartland of the Iveses? Granted she had not meant to hit old Aunt Trudy in the bulkhead, still she knew that Sam practiced general medicine in Westhampton and that they all lived there year round. She intended to announce herself absolutely. She would not leave their meeting to chance. On the very evening Frank told her he'd heard the church wanted to sell this property it was settled. In a split second she turned about-face, excited to pick up all the stitches from the past, all of them. Her old love of Billie burst the bonds. Sam she could scarcely recollect, not her lust for him or her humiliation, and from the time she got wind, first in Billie's letters and then through Robbie's conjecturing, that it was a bad marriage, what was left of her grievances dropped away. She wouldn't mind seeing Sam at all now.

There was a jet-settish cast to Billie's life and it is probably not to be wondered too much that the roaming Robbie would roam into her by chance on some unlikely shore. It was a damned unlikely shore, as it turned out, the shore of the Nile below a Nubian village where they watched through the night as their tourist yacht burned to the waterline. The yacht, with forty passengers and twenty crew, belonged to the Egyptian government and had been returning from one of its last scheduled visits to Abu Simbel at its old site. The fire, later attributed to an act of God, took two lives, and many people were injured. Robbie said that he had noticed the Iveses on the trip up but hadn't actually met them. They had been in a party of beautiful people. However, in the press of the disaster they sorted themselves out and quickly came to the top, Sam through his natural authority as physician, Billie from natural humanity and competence. It had been music, he said, just to watch her as she caught the measure of the stately black Nubian women, moving to their rhythm, long-limbed, quiet, comforting people, finding pallets and food, and whatever materials might be improvised for Sam's use. As Sam's nurse she never flinched. It was the next year that some of the survivors had a reunion at Stresa. Sam hadn't been able to make it. Robbie and Billie climbed on yet another yacht—to conquer a fear of yachts, probably —and cruised Lake Maggiore for days, or weeks. Robbie had

visited the Iveses in Westhampton a few times since. He
didn't like Sam.

"It's a question whether Sam will drown in alcohol or self-
pity," Robbie had said. "But I have some sympathy for him,
some little sympathy. He believes if he could just have his
wife waiting quietly and alone in the evening with his slip-
pers the way other wives do, or should, or he thinks they
should—he has a banal mind—they would be happy. As it is,
she keeps herself safely in the center of a horde of children
and squatting hippies and foreign emigré houseguests, some
with titles. Her need to be surrounded is acute and she is not
too discriminating. There's a lot of free-loading in that household, but of course there's a lot of money to support it. She
even travels in a swarm.

"I'll tell you a story I think of when I see her. In Arabia
once I heard about a doctor who had set up a clinic for
women in a particularly backward sultanate. The women had
had absolutely no medical attention and the clinic was a
radical innovation, and it was a question who was the more
daring, the doctor or the frightened wives who sneaked in to
see him. Each one came in with her head in a cloud of buzz-
ing flies. It was the custom to set their hair in camel dung and
the flies lived in it, you see, so they all came in together. They
were an ecological unit, you see? But the great thing was that
when the woman left, her flies left with her."

"And that's Billie."

"And that's Billie. When you're with her inevitably you're
only one of several flies. Sam has his whisky, of course. But
it doesn't come out evenly. It's Billie's dung, they're Billie's
flies. Sam's no match for them."

This picture of Sam so nicely reduced him as to be somebody Erica might easily and kindly greet.

Erica finished her sparrow grass and now prepared to greet
easily and kindly her husband. He and Lucy, the older of
her two children, who had finished her first year at Smith,

were driving out from the city in time for dinner. They would need three hours to make the two-hour trip from the North Bronx. Aside from the strain of traffic, Frank would have to endure the strain of Lucy, who upon discovering women's liberation stopped being his darling daughter and started being a pain in the neck. Always a verbal child, she now sprayed her papa with buckshot: What proportion of the university faculty were women, and how many full professors? (Four.) And how many associates? (One.) And did he know that in Boston, a city of X million people, not one woman was a full partner in a law firm? Her papa, whose field was justice and who worked in a New York City university, did not really need a revolutionary daughter of statistics to awaken him to the social inequities in America. When he became dean he assumed the role of protector of women and girls from being mugged and raped. It was very hard for him to listen to the idea that while women and girls did not want to be mugged and raped, they did not love him for assuming the role of protector. Moreover, finding Robbie in Moriches was going to make his cheek twitch.

Sure enough, when Erica heard the car she went down the driveway to intercept a red-headed daughter with a brow that was stormy and a husband with a cheek that twitched. She kissed the brow and put her hand up to smooth the cheek.

"Hello girl," he said gently. "That Robbie's car with the Massachusetts plate?"

"He's staying on. He's our liaison man with the Iveses," she answered just as gently.

"Fine," said Frank. "It'll be good to see the bastard again. Does Billie know you're here yet?" He was very keen to have Erica revive her relationship with the Iveses, but not to have his brother be a party to it.

"I put a note in the evening mail." They walked to the house side by side, she feeling, disloyally, like a little post commander briefing their terrific general. They'd all been at their ease through the week and now they'd all look sharp. He made a damn good-looking general, broadened from a boy to a man, and stood up straight, which Lucy didn't do, and was fit. He could beat up any one of them. Erica reported conditions on the base, commending everybody for their good behavior. Frank nodded and nodded and went up to wash.

On the shady east side of the house under the trees was a wide screened porch where they so far chose to live their indoor life. It was where they ate, as it gave off the kitchen, where some napped, and now they were drinking there. Frank came down smiling, refreshed, paused at the threshold, gave a warm greeting to his mother-in-law, who loved him but thought he was uxorious, to Honora and Simon, whom he loved, and held out his hand, narrowed his narrow eyes, and said, "Robbie, glad you could stay. Ma's all right?" Ma was fine, still crocheting bedsocks for the elderly on St. Polycarp's Christmas list.

"Jesus, I tried to get up there all spring," said Frank, "but it was a terrible year *before* Cambodia . . . and *afterward* . . . and then the strike. Literally, this is the first moment I've felt it wasn't absolutely foolhardy to leave the campus for more than a few hours."

"Well, she does keep herself tucked away in an inconvenient slum," said Robbie.

"What kind of a crack is that?" Frank shot back. "I've been trying to get her out of there since Pa died."

"I know you have, old boy. She's bullheaded. I know you have," said Robbie in a lulling voice.

They went on to the neutral ground of Vietnam but then Lucy, who was a field marshaless in that other war, women's liberation, insisted upon sharing with them the latest development on that front: it had been proved that the nuclear family had to be very corrupt because by confining women to a secondary position it forced them to use their immense energy and intelligence *deviously*.

Her father said, "That's quite a generalization, Lucy," with commendable patience, having no doubt been over this terrain a lot of times between New York and Moriches. But Frank was very good with the young. He was known for it.

"It may be a generalization, Frank," said Ellen to her son-in-law, "but if I had stayed home, it would have corrupted me. It would have turned me into a stage mother." And then as an afterthought she said, "Erica's marvelous."

"I know, of course," said Frank, "that academic life is a world apart. Our women are the peers of their men. Erica and I aren't an exception. And she can tell you there isn't an article I write or an idea I have that I don't want to talk over with her first and foremost."

This was true but it made Erica feel like Dr. Johnson's dog, and she got up on her own hind legs and said, "Faculty wives are adjunctive, Frank, and if the women are peers, they're devious peers . . . a lot of them."

"Why do you say that? Why do you say that, Erica?" Frank asked in the slightly wounded voice he used with unhappy undergraduates. "You or Frances or Margaret, not one of you is devious. You're all independent, equal, respected women."

"Oh, we know a lot of colonel's ladies, Frank, you know that. And as to contented peers, it seems to me dissatisfaction among the younger wives starts earlier and is more extensive than ever it used to be. After all, the point is their dignity is derivative. And so is mine," she said gently. "I paper over the cracks. But really what I am is a kind of . . . stage manager. I don't mind, you know. I like staying home and doing the house . . . but it's still true that we all expect . . . me . . . to provide the most attractive background I can to set . . . you . . . off to greatest advantage."

"You've been magnificent!" Frank said grandly. "You're

absolutely right to take the credit. There's nobody more gracious than you are and I wouldn't be where I am without you. It hasn't anything at all to do with inequality."

"Nonsense, Frank," said Robbie, sounding quiet and reasonable as the devil. "It has everything to do with inequality. It's in the structure. The American university is unequal in all its parts and, to borrow the language of the law, *you* have to be tainted. Your situation may of course be an exception, but among the people I know in academic life in Boston and Cambridge, I would have to say that a lot of women, even those who have independent work"—and here he paused and thought and pushed his hair back and said deliberately —"I'd have to say the women mount the men."

"The female doesn't mount the male, old boy! That's not how it's done!" Frank trumped him, and twitch went his cheek. He would not believe that his brother's words had been deliberate.

Chapter 12

One could not see through the lilac hedge to the neighboring cottage. A plank fence running from the water to the road was hidden in it. Erica, with a bottle of burgundy and a note attached, had to walk up to the road and around. It was the following morning. She wore a bottle-green dress under the bottle-green pines that were dripping from a finished rain. The day had already slipped from her control. There were uncertainties. It was uncertain how warm would be Aunt Trudy's greeting after twenty years of studied neglect, whether Billie would call when she got the letter, whether Frank would slug Robbie before evening. From the road the little cottage was just as privately hedged as the mother house, and Erica had never seen it. She let herself in through a white-painted wooden gate and there it was, cozy in its cozy quarter acre, grey-shingled with white trim, and hugged by tea roses. It was partly sheltered from the public dock beyond it by a weathered split-rail fence bunted with more roses, deep red ones; roses, roses, the right thing out here.

There wasn't a soul anywhere, not even an old man fishing from the public dock.

The water twinkled, Erica blinked and was suddenly frightened to be seen trespassing. In a nervous quiet, she followed the curve of the path to the front porch to put her wine offering on a box settle on the porch. Unaccountably, her knees wobbled and she sat down. It was so still, so empty of any sign of life except for the far-off dots of boats, that it amazed her to be certain there was somebody inside the house. She listened. Propped rigid against the settle, she strained to catch the sound of nothing. She believed that if she got up and left calmly they would shoot her right in the back. Then immediately there were footsteps and somebody wrestling with the door. It opened and out came a deep-tanned fair-headed man in a faded black jersey, chinos, sneakers, who was unquestionably Sam. She stood up. Behind her large dark glasses she was questionably Erica.

"My God, you scared the . . . Erica?" he said in the hush of astonishment.

"Yes," she said, shy from being caught out. Her surprise wasn't in a class with his. She knew she was prowling in the neighborhood of his life but he didn't. "If you had had time to read your morning mail I . . . would not be inexplicable."

"Erica, Erica—hell, you are the best person I've ever known in my life. I'm so glad to see you back!" He gave her a hug and then impetuously another, and kissed her on both cheeks, and a hundred pullulating shoots and buds of pleasure quickened her to life. She flushed and said, "I didn't see a car . . . I just wanted to . . ."

"I've got my boat tied up over there," he said, nodding to the town pier. "Let me look at you . . . Jesus, it's been years since one of life's surprises has been good. The shock may kill me. How the *hell* can you be here?" And not waiting for her to say how the hell, he went on in a quiet rush of breath, "Take off your glasses and let me see you properly. I didn't know you had green eyes. . . . Good God, you're making me cry . . . this calls for . . . don't move. Sit down on your white bench in your green dress. I'll be back in half a minute."

To be greeted by somebody with such extravagant joy was not an unpleasant experience. Erica sat thoughtless on the white settle in a state of giddy happiness. Sam came back with two glasses. She said, "Whisky for breakfast?" He said, "I bet you think you're the only one on this porch for George McGovern!"

"Oh Sam," she said, beaming. "I'm so glad to hear you say that."

It was the True Sign even to have heard of McGovern's candidacy, and Erica was delighted by it the more for its being the echo of the one moment in their old romance she could remember without wincing. Sam, however, seemed to revel in a kind of total recall. The sight of Erica brought back to him a flood of grievances he'd suffered that year—about how his father had been determined to break his will and make him be a doctor, and how his mother said if he became a writer she would be forced to have a nervous breakdown. The memory of how shabbily he had treated Erica seemed, however, to have been totally erased.

She sat back on the settle and smiled and blinked happily like Sleeping Beauty—actually more like her grandfather— and allowed Sam's outpouring to pass for full repentance. She didn't have to talk at all, it was clear. All she had to do was listen. Sam's sunburned face was a pleasure to look at, healthy, wealthy, and wise, made wise by a trick of fine white lines at his eyes. He was losing the golden hair on his high forehead, but skin taut over a man's well-shaped skull was very attractive to Erica. She watched the pulse beat at his temple while he talked and found it curiously touching, and it made her think of the oyster in the spine of a turkey, which was even more curious. He was certainly a far cry from the lank-locked Ryans.

"I've got a secret vice," Sam said, smiling confidently at

her. He could be confident. It was easy, easy. It was easy for him to be handsome. "Years ago I got into the habit of flipping through every new issue of *Whitewood's* magazine to see if you were in." It was easy for Erica to like him. He admired her articles enormously. She did not hazard saying, well, for instance, which one? She didn't ask did he happen to run across her books? She murmured that lately she was in some distress because of not being able to write. He wouldn't hear of it! She had the perfect life, absolutely. And it suited her. She looked absolutely great. *Really*. He meant it.

Well, really, she felt it. "I must return the compliment," she said. "You are handsomer than ever. You must have an enormous obstetrical practice."

"I refused to take it!" said Sam, and his voice dropped thunk! an octave and he tucked in his chin. "They expect you to subsist on four hours of sleep a night. Well, they had to find somebody else to. . . . You can't imagine how demanding women are these days . . . and spoiled—they're not prepared to tolerate any pain at all . . . or else they're natural childbirth fanatics and expect you to hold their hand for . . . I drew the line. No obstetrics, no house calls."

"None at all?" she asked, unsure by now whether she was enchanted or disenchanted.

"Oh, of course I make *some* house calls. When I hear the necessity for it, of course I go. If it were up to Billie I'd be driving ten miles to take out a splinter. I can hear an awful lot on the phone, Erica. After all, my professional judgment is worth *some*thing. I have an ear for hysteria. I can discount it. Usually if it's really serious they're better off getting right into the hospital where there's . . . but Billie . . . I'd have a coronary before I was fifty if . . ."

So Billie entered the conversation, however inauspiciously. And Sam was not looking pretty when she did. He had allowed his expression to collapse in such aggrieved folds of flesh as to remind Erica of a carved pumpkin after two weeks' sitting on the stoop. It embarrassed her to see the boyish petulance in his middle-aged face and she wondered at his letting it show. She didn't like to look.

"I can't wait to see Billie again. It's been twenty years, Sam," she said, getting up from the bench as though she would not wait another minute more. They went inside to put away the glasses. It was a maple-rocker and hooked-rug cottage, and as her eyes became accustomed to the light she could pick out some of Aunt Trudy's old possessions, above all a large daguerreotype of two Hansel and Gretel-y children in an olden wood holding hands and unaccountably wearing saddle shoes. "Oh Sam," she said, delighted. "I remember that picture so well. I couldn't get over their shoes because . . ."

"Goddamit, the phone's not connected yet! I spoke to Stebbins last week about it. She's going to blow her top if they haven't fixed her favorite toy."

"Well, come round to my house and you can call, and you can call Billie, too, won't you? How is she? Still very beautiful, I hear."

"Billie needs a keel," he said sternly. "She's always needed a keel."

"Let's see," said Erica, trying another tack, "Your oldest boy, Mark, must be nineteen. What is he doing?"

"Doing? Absolutely nothing. Living off the fat of my back! He hasn't enough character to make a good hippie. Hardly surprising, of course, when she never expected anything of the boys, wouldn't discipline them . . ." He was back in an angry sulk but caught himself. His face cleared, he resumed being handsome, and he said, "Green is your color. Is that why you married an Irishman?" When he was bad he was very very bad, but when he was good he beguiled Erica.

They closed the cottage and side by side strolled out of one property and down the driveway of the other. Sam talked about tennis, tuitions, air fares, jibed at his life in a

radical sheikdom, and concluded with shocking inconsis-
tency that, as lots went, he had the best of it. They were approaching the house when, with an easy yielding to a seeming impulse, he put his arm around her shoulder, pulled her
to him sideways, and kissed her hair. It sent a sizzle through
Erica along with the thought of how, if they all saw it, they
would account for such familiarity from a stranger.

Not *all* of them saw it. On the instant of the kiss, Honora
came bolting down the kitchen stairs yelling, "There you are,
Mama! We've been looking every place," while a car had entered the driveway right behind them with Simon at the
wheel, and Erica could see the silhouette of Robbie sitting
on the screen porch, surely watching. It was very gratifying
to think she had thrown the lot of them. She was the last person they would have credited with an untold story. Honora
shook hands with Sam and said that her father was upset because he'd got a call and had to go back to the city. He was
looking for clean laundry.

Frank came out to greet them and be delighted to hear
who Sam was. Frank, tall, well-groomed, cordial, was Erica's
attribute now. She scanned the face of the attribute for anxiety about his call from New York but it was all assurance,
all command.

"Oh this damned open-admissions business," he answered
with some elaboration of detail and the mention of many
important people. He was lying. He was a truthful person
who made a terrible liar. There was no moral in that. She
was a truthful person who made a good liar. They went out
to the porch, where Robbie said he was glad to see Sam
again, and *he* was lying. They sat down, all of them, the
three men with their legs crossed, each with a fine long
thigh and calf and a foot pointing to the middle, Erica upright, her head in the clouds. She was taken by the memory
of an earlier circle when they played spin-the-bottle in the
old chicken house. But now there was a wonderful reversal

of her situation. Now in this circle she was twelve noon, and the focus of a sexual tension unprecedented in her experience. Of course, not counting Frank at all.

It was Robbie foremost. He was roused by Erica's arousal although he must have found soft Sam's being the cause of it at the very least ironic. But while it was true that Sam was the cause, it wasn't a sexual response to *him* that had Erica blooming. What he gave her now, and he had done it once before, was a sense of her own female identity, an earthy believability. He made her feel that if the layers of Western civilization were peeled off Erica T. Ryan, there would still be a solid woman left and everybody would want to drag her to his cave. This was a rare musky voluptuous feeling which she enjoyed at the expense of her good sense. She looked from Robbie, who watched her covertly, to Sam, who gave her an intimate smile of approval, to Frank, who talked and talked, and she felt superb.

The talk was smart. Frank matched with his wit every dollar Sam had. Social parity was established by the proud trading of points against their women: what the hell they were going to do with all the inherited fur coats they wouldn't wear? Send them to Biafra? To the welfare mothers? Sam said that the cost of Billie's flying to Paris for a wool one every year would . . . and in fact the cost of supporting Billie in *all* her various revolutionary causes . . . although what really sent him up a wall was women's liberation . . . that Billie had the face to discover all of a sudden that she was a sex object. Jesus . . .

But good old Frank had to demur here. He had to defend his Erica, his Rock of Gibraltar. In your wildest dreams you wouldn't mistake her for a sex object. Their Lucy was into women's liberation.

Robbie sniffed and rallied. "I'll tell you what I find interesting," he said. "I find it interesting to see the curiously brutal use man has made of his sentimentalizing women and children. One can find evidence of how pervasive the subjugation of women . . ."

"It has seemed to me an insult to the mind, old boy, to hear women borrow the rhetoric of cruelly oppressed people like the blacks and the Puerto Ricans," said Frank bang-bang, disqualifying the evidence or quashing the indictment or Robbie.

"You've missed the whole point of the women's movement, old boy," Robbie said in a matter-of-fact way, but Sam, thank God, said, "Jesus Christ, I forgot the time! Do you mind if I use your phone?" Frank led him off, and Erica and Robbie sat on in silence, each for a damn good reason. They could overhear ". . . delayed by an emergency . . . another hour, at least" and ". . . that phone is still *out*. I believe, Mr. Stebbins, that I may lay claim to having more pressing matters to attend to than the reconnection of public utilities . . ."

The importance of being Sam had not been lost on Erica, and she wondered whether Billie was going to divorce him. When he'd hung up she had said, "Do, Sam, call Billie," but he said he was late as hell as it was, that with this wind he'd be delayed more than an hour and his office hours began at one, and then, *sotto voce,* "We've got to talk, Ric. I've got to see you. Alone. Privately. For old time's sake . . ."

He left and she watched him through the screen. When he was out of earshot she groaned in happy relief, the groan of somebody who had missed the boat and then heard the boat went down. She had had trouble not seeing that Sam was superficial when she was a girl in love, but afterward her fancy designed him at will to suit a broken heart or her wounded self-esteem. To have him return in the flesh, and in the flesh that was clearly weak, was to have an old question resolved. She smiled fondly across the bay.

Robbie had been watching the watcher and remarked quizzically, "I had no idea you knew Sam."

Erica, miles away in time and space, was jarred by Robbie's voice and said, "And now you have?" in a tone that was just and correct. It was a correction for baiting Frank, and therein lay the justice. Justice is sometimes circular. Robbie gave a little nod and left the porch and Erica was at once dismayed and ashamed by the powers let loose in her.

If Sam had made Erica a little more interesting in Robbie's eyes, a little more enigmatic—something she had certainly never been, enigmatic—he did not in her husband's eyes. She found Frank upstairs, full of zest, packing a suitcase on their bed. He checked through the laundry and he checked through his wife:

"I hate to leave you again, my poor Ric . . . with a houseful of boarders. . . . Make the girls help you more . . . they're certainly old enough . . ." A pause for decision about shirts. "Well, with Sam Ives we have a doctor in the family out here . . . handy. I thought he was attractive, decent enough. . . . What did you think? I must say, my brother didn't cut much of a figure in his capacity as liaison man, did he? I don't see any handkerchiefs . . . oh, here they are. . . . Do you know that I haven't slept in this bed three times? Nobody will be happier to see a few things resolved than I. But my poor girl, it's very hard on you, putting this house together by yourself. You've done a great job. It's looking wonderful . . . I've been hoping it would cheer you up a little. I'd like to see you feel better."

But Erica thought she hadn't felt better in her life. And it seemed to her neither had he. So taken up was she by her own secret joys she forgot to ask him whatever was it he had been lying about before.

Chapter 13

When Frank went back to the city it was like lifting the glass. Erica's boarders scattered like beetles in a beetle race. She had looked for Robbie to make it up with him, but Ellen on her own way out said he had left with the message they weren't to wait supper. It was deflating. Already past two and Billie hadn't phoned. That was deflating. Erica waved her arms through the empty downstairs rooms and went up to wash and to find in the bathroom mirror some friendly confirmation that her soul was lightened and enlightened. She was just smiling encouragingly when a car door banged and she went off to Lucy's window to see who the hell was coming back so soon. But it was Billie coming back after twenty years.

The two women ran into each other's arms, hugged and laughed and had tears in their eyes and Billie said over and over, "I can't believe it! I can't believe it!" They agreed that each looked exactly the same only incredibly much better, and they meant it with two full hearts. Billie, in a short

white tennis dress, hadn't washed, had come in from the
courts, found Erica's letter, drove off without her license,
was starving, was stupefied, could not under*stand* why Erica
had refused to see her, what was the reason? What had she
done? This refusal through all these years had hovered
above her like an awful judgment, "a black sign like the
sight of a flock of starlings. I never had the right, I know
. . . I never was entitled to expect your unflagging devotion
. . . nothing like that, I *know* . . . but how could I have
merited . . . there were times when I craved to talk to you
. . . it isn't that I haven't got lots of friends . . . Erica,
you've got to tell me what I did because I know I didn't do
it!" This beautiful Amazon with the freckles and the nose
peeling, with her sun glasses as big as saucers pushed on
top of her stubby pale yellow hair, burst into tears and fell
into Erica's arms again. Two half-sisters made one whole,
Erica thought, and remembered thinking wistfully often and
often. She was deeply dumfounded. She stared back along
the trail of misery she had witlessly laid and her mind rico-
cheted in belief and disbelief. She put an arm around Billie's
waist and they walked around to the front porch, and she
said in a soft moan, "It wasn't you at all . . . let's get something to eat . . . it was altogether me, my problem . . ."

"Do you remember," said Billie, "how we once sat on this
step in the rain?"

"I remember everything."

In the kitchen Billie gripped a glass decanter of red wine
by its throat and said that was all she wanted. Erica said
they had to have some cheese at least. Frank had brought
some good French bread out from New York, and some
Jarlsberg, and it was Erica's policy to eat wisely right
through the most dramatic emotional crises. "That's what I
mean, Ric! How many times when I was falling apart you
could have put me together again with bread and cheese!"

"Oh Billie," Erica sighed, part bewildered, part chagrined,

"I was always thinking of you and longing to see you. But you seemed to have such a self-sufficient spirit. I never thought of your seriously missing me. I only thought it was my sentence."

They took their wine and bread and cheese back to the top porch step, two very unlike-looking women, more so than ever they were when they last sat there: one expensive, breezy, long-legged, blue-eyed, the early mischief in her face now hardened into defiance, the other in a dark green dress, feeling just average. This day was unlike the earlier day as well, with the clearest air, the truest color, the water choppy and turning black. Erica told how she had met Sam that morning, how she had discovered Billie's mother would be her neighbor. Billie couldn't believe anything. Then they accounted for each other, for their children, politics, tastes, husbands, their stations in the world and their private time.

It was an introductory accounting, neither one of them intending to bowdlerize her life so much as to lend a seemly modesty to the overall story of it, and this was not because either Erica or Billie was roused to compete for place, but rather to put on things the best-mannered face, to begin with, out of a considerate respect for the many people they represented. Erica came very close to establishing herself as just the average American housewife, and Billie was just the average American housewife too, albeit one who skied in the Andes and went scuba diving in the Red Sea. Billie was the mother of boys, and boys looked right for Billie. There were five of them ranging from nineteen to eleven, and they all played tennis and were very sensitive. The sixth child was a girl of eight whose name was Moira and was her father's love. Sam never seemed able to let the boys express their individual natures the way he let Moira express hers. My God, she did express hers! Goodness, didn't Erica know what a father was like about daughters! Frank was unabashedly child-proud.

So they talked, but even in this preliminary draft of who they were it was clear that what was going on underneath in the way of hardship and reverses was very far removed from a homelife suggested by Billie's Boys and Little Women. The amount of sensitivity in Billie's household was so rich as to seem alarmingly to have disabled most of its members. Her boys began dropping out of nursery school. There was no question about Billie's motherly investment or her anxiety for her young, but in spite of it, or to rest from it, she spent a lot of her year lying on her back under the sun of some other continent.

Erica, twist her own tale as she tried, reported herself out a heavily wholesome woman constantly rewarded by success. She and Frank were wonderfully suited, she explained, and didn't know a moment of serious strain. She knew they were awfully lucky.

"I've cause to think it is true that marriages are made in the unconscious and answer one's unsuspected needs," Erica said. In fact, it was something she *used* to think. Now she might equally have said she was having cause to believe that her unsuspected needs had not been answered.

"I think you may be extrapolating from a series of one," Billie replied.

Erica hesitated but her insight into her present restlessness was scattered and blurry and after a pause she fell back upon a truth that had since been superseded. "Well, I seem to be that rare thing, a contented woman. I don't feel complacent. Really, it seems like the wildest chance that I would find domestic life so satisfying. I guess it was like flinging Br'er Rabbit into the briar patch. But now . . . I've come to a sort of watershed. Lucy's at Smith, Honora's a most independent child. I can do all the familial business off the top of my head and it's time for me . . . to be a separate entity . . . to insist to myself that my profession claim me as wholly as if I were a man. And there's the rub. Suppose

my profession to be writing, I can't write. I *can not* write
. . . it's a mute and inglorious crisis but it's mine . . . and
it's got me down." She smiled and looked at Billie's intent,
sympathetic face, and went on in a mildly self-mocking tone,
"*However,* I have not been a Pollyana all these years without learning a few tricks. I'm not happy when I'm down. In
my desperation to get up again I would sell my soul for a
mess of pottage, *gladly.* The problem, of course, is to find
a buyer. But I think I might have one. I haven't told anybody but Frank about it—not even Robbie, my confessor—
but I've gone to *Whitewood's* magazine to ask for a full-
time job doing editorial work. They seem to be taking me
fairly seriously . . . two interviews—but they're a subsid-
iary now, they aren't in complete control of their own policy
—it's complicated . . . anyway, I run for the mail every
morning . . . we'll see."

"Would you be an editor?"

"Yes."

"Well, wouldn't that be marvelous?" Billie said in a voice
inviting a little more enthusiasm. She might make a cheer-
leader and wouldn't even have to change her dress, Erica
thought, but she said, "Yes, only I don't like to edit. I don't
like to touch anybody else's work."

"Well, if you're helplessly terrific at everything you'll
probably be terrific at that," Billie said, smiling and still
cheering her on.

They had been talking for nearly two hours when Erica
asked did Billie think they should check if her mother had
arrived, but Billie said absolutely not. They left the porch
and walked slowly the perimeter of the lawn, along the lilac
hedge through which, if you were nuns, you couldn't be
seen, and if you were Aunt Trudy she couldn't see you. And
then they walked along the retaining wall, where they
checked for dead bodies and crabs. They came to the chairs
under the butternut tree by the creek mouth where the

tide was changing and the water slapped about every which way with no proper direction. They sat down and finally and inevitably Billie asked, "What was the sentence for? Why did you have to impose a sentence?"

Erica had no absolute moral rule against lying. She did not, however, like it as an art form and rarely resorted to it. She had had time on the porch step to consider the handling of this question that Billie was certain to ask. Through their halting walk from the house together there had been lawn enough and time. A moment's panic might have been allowed her at finding herself on the spot, the particular spot she had been so gymnastically clever at avoiding being put on. She might have resolved a dilemma by saying, "Billie, I can't tell you."

"I had fallen in love with Sam, you see," is what she said. "It was as simple as that." After all, it was such an old story to Erica and of no moment now that she found she could deliver her confession easily and it even sounded a little silly. She did expect to hear Billie again astonished and say again she couldn't believe it, she couldn't believe it, but Billie, in her refreshing strange way, seemed easily able to believe it.

"So that was it!" Billie said. "What a tempest in a teapot!" And she asked how and when and where out of an amused curiosity without any sign of being shaken by a revelation. They were logistical questions and Erica gave geographical answers . . . well, they had of course met at the party in Quogue, and then he had come up to Northampton to see her, and she had gone down to New York . . .

"Good heavens," said Billie very fondly, "it's a tale told by an idiot."

"At the *time*, Billie, you have to remember how we were all feeling at the *time*," Erica protested. Her reaction at the time hadn't been awfully inflated.

"Poor Erica, you were always more sinned against than

sinning," Billie sighed. "I bet you never even slept with him."

"Oh yes I did," Erica admitted, and broke into a laugh. "Once." They both laughed.

"Twenty years! My God, that's a stiff sentence for one simple little . . . Erica, my poor baby, I wonder you didn't stitch a scarlet letter to your gym suit."

It occurred to Erica all at once, in one of those rare illuminating connections, that while peripherally she was honest, with the world she was honest, at the core with herself she was neither honest nor dishonest. When it came to a painful or uncomfortable question of what she really thought, or what she really wanted, she was in the habit of shunting it off, of finding the answer in what she ought to think and ought to want. Not Billie. Billie could lie her head off to anybody if she saw the need, but she never confused herself. Erica emerged from confusion with a need of her own.

"Listen, Billie, I wonder if I have the right to ask you a favor? I would be distressed if Sam were to know that I told you. After all, he never gave me away."

"Nothing could be easier," she said. "I don't tell him anything. We hardly exchange two words a week."

A car door slammed, and then another. "When I hear the slam of two car doors I think the posse's coming to get me," Erica said. "Well, weren't we awfully lucky to have had this private time?"

They were lucky. They gathered themselves together and stood their ground under the tree waiting for whoever would be coming round the curve of the house. As Erica knew it was a bang too many for Robbie, she didn't mind in what order they all came home again. Two more slams, another posse, they came not in single spies but in battalions. Ellen with one daughter, Simon with another. So the half-sisters set off thick as thieves across the grass to take them on. Just before the two sides joined and while they were still out of earshot, Billie said to Erica, "It explains a lot, it explains a lot. When I was in Edinburgh and my mother wrote that you were married to Frank Ryan I thought, Well, even good Erica Thoroughgood has to do what everybody else has to do. Tuck tail. It explains a lot."

Chapter 14

Erica steered Billie straight to her car through a great deal of family cordiality. It seemed nobody knew where Billie was, not her children, who were accustomed not to know, nor her houseguests, who, Erica suspected, might have been years searching the world for a kind of Commune Hilton and tumbled happily upon it at the Iveses', nor did old Aunt Trudy know, who had expected to be greeted by her daughter in midafternoon at the door of her rosy rented cottage. Clearly, Billie was untroubled by the lot of them. Erica said she would defer the experience of yet another reunion until the next day and did not go around with Billie to see her mother. The half-sisters divided for the time.

Erica went off to the kitchen to put to simmer the lamb stew she had made because Robbie liked it but would not be there to eat. Through dinner she saved her own simmering and stewing until she could be alone again. The conversation was all Ives, all hearty and approving. Erica kept half an ear alert for the return of Robbie.

Upstairs in her room she regarded the great matrimonial

bed with ambivalence. Frank had said he hadn't slept in it three times. Accurate enough. He had slept in it twice. Every sort of violence, organized and disorganized, consequent upon the excelerating dissolution of American society had an active chapter at the university in this worst year in the life of the republic. Frank had stood by with his cool head, his wit, his sympathy for the young and the blacks, always lending at least his bodily presence.

In September he had made hospital rounds at the infirmary because of a series of bad muggings and then the rape of a teaching assistant; a grim beginning. Thereafter he began taking a night walk through the school by himself, rain or clear, with the fidelity of an old postman. Erica offered to keep him company but he said no. Every night after dark, varying his time and his route, he walked alone under the trees in the lamplight. He was looking out for everybody. And everybody was looking out for him. The consequence was a near disappearance of wanton violence on their campus. But then in May there was Cambodia. Anyway, Frank had been selfless. The university felt itself immensely lucky to have Dean Ryan in a time perilously short of heroes. There were some holdouts who said Frank Ryan thought he was Bobby Kennedy and the Mayor, that no matter how thin you sliced him . . . so therefore, not surprisingly, he had slept in the new bed in the new house only twice.

Erica was standing at the foot of this matrimonial bed in a brown study when there was a knock at her door and it was Honora.

"Mama, is something the matter?"

"No, no. I'm just pensive."

"We couldn't find you anyplace. Uncle Robbie called and said to tell you he's in Boston looking in on Grandma Ryan and that he'll be back sooner or later."

"Boston? Goodness, whatever came over him to go up to Boston?"

"I asked him and he said he found himself over at Orient Point and thought it was a nice day for a ferry ride."

"Didn't he ask to speak to me?"

"No. He just said what I said." Honora was still uncertain and wanted her mother to be reassuringly moodless. "Aren't you coming downstairs, Mama? I've got a box of Butterfingers I'm willing to let you watch me eat." She had her father's jaw, which she used for her comic acts.

"I'm coming right down," said her mother, smiling, unable to resist her child.

Erica brought her book down to the screened porch, where Simon sat behind his newspaper and Lucy was deep into *Sexual Politics*, about which they were all certain to hear a good deal. She opened to her place in *A Room of One's Own* and let her mind run loose over the day. Her flesh had been pinched to life by Sam and her spirit by Billie. She made a little mental tour of her meeting with Sam and hoped once and for all she might be free of all the tiny Sam-generated, Sam-associated, Sam-derived assumptions of inadequacy that had left her faintly apologetic about being alive. But it was the restoration of the old hard-hearted realistic and fundamentally uncapitulating Billie to her romantic place in the scheme of things that left Erica musing deeply. The business about tucking tail, that fresh shot at such an ancient event— really an act of exhumation—well, it was marvelous how Billie pulled the past into the present. She suspended time. It was all laid out before them, what they did as girls and who they were now. It was as if tucking tail and marrying Frank Ryan wasn't history. It was as if every successful flourishing thing that happened to Erica since . . . did not necessarily prove she had made a wise choice.

She had tucked tail. Before she married Frank she used to call him a trimmer but afterward she never did. She had just slipped under his chin, she had relinquished in one sweep her combative independent *indifference* to whatever it was in his thinking, and in himself, that she didn't like. *Of course* she relinquished her indifference. That was marriage. Into the bargain she had thrown in the possibilities for a separate development and became, in the classical manner, her husband's better self. That gave him two selves, or at least more than one. Right on her lap she could put her finger on Virginia Woolf's words, "Women have served all these centuries as looking glasses, possessing the magic and delicious power of reflecting the figure of a man at twice its natural size." It was the size Frank liked best.

But how was it possible to say to a man who has been spending all his waking hours at attempts to redress the enormous inequities of the social system, "Look here, I would like to ask you to examine a few small but patronizing assumptions you make about me that I have begun not to be able to bear?" Erica would not do it. However, as the princess in question, that was where the pea lay and she knew it and Robbie knew it.

And where was Robbie, her relief, her supply minister, her closet brother with whom she was accustomed to touch upon her secret doubts no matter how intimate—about the consequences of a low-protein diet to rural Mississippi and the South Bronx, or about Britain's entry into the Common Market, which she publicly favored but *privately* . . . and even whether she ought not to approach Lucy about choosing the IUD over the pill, although never about her marriage.

"Robbie is such an attractive person," said Ellen, who had wandered onto the porch with nothing to read, startling her daughter. "It always seems to me too sad that he's one of those men who is suspended in a sort of limbo for life by the unthinking demands of a self-centered women."

"What do you mean, Ellen?" her daughter asked severely.

"Oh, you know," said Ellen. "The sort of woman who thoughtlessly and indefinitely detains a man who might otherwise have been free to make other relationships. It

seems to me obvious that his mother's been rather shabby
with him."

It was an understandable relief to Erica that her mother-
in-law was in the dock, and she could be generous: "I don't
know that Robbie doesn't use her even in his own mind as
an excuse for not taking on . . . oh, you know, the encum-
brances of marriage. He doesn't live with her, after all. He
has rooms of his own. He's a man who likes to keep loose.
No doubt he's very grateful to his mother for allowing the
world to account to her for his never marrying."

"Well, possibly," Ellen said skeptically. "These private
people sometimes have a private life . . . I wouldn't be surprised to hear he's had a great love. . . . What do you think,
Simon?"

"I think having a great love is to be recommended," Simon
said mildly from behind the *Times,* and Erica heard him with
one dart of jealousy over Robbie and one of envy for her
mother. Ellen had known a great love, and in fact probably
two, and if Ellen talked about a self-centered woman she
knew whereof she spoke in that regard as well. Erica thought
her mother must have been wildly in love with her father
when she married him and wildly out of love inside a year.
Her contentment with Simon had long been obvious. Clearly
Ellen was the sort of woman who lived with a man she loved,
or she left him. Not every daughter had such a model of integrity to reflect upon.

Next morning Erica confronted an altogether different
proposition in the way of mothers. She went up the driveway and around to greet Billie's, feeling reduced to a child
who knew it had been naughty for about twenty years and
would be called upon to make some small accounting. Well,
she thought, I'm Billie's half-sister but I'm just Trudy's
quarter-daughter. In her memory her Aunt Trudy was large
and blooming and with her thick-plaited fair hair something
like a foreign doll without the white apron but with a bad

temper. It had already been forced upon her attention that people do not mellow the way they are supposed to and, in fact, whatever they were they tend to become more so. And so it ought not to have been a surprise to find Aunt Trudy right there in the middle of that bell curve. She welcomed Erica in full plaint.

"Erica Thoroughgood, a mother of grown children! When I read your note! How you bring back the happy years! You'll never be anything but Erica Thoroughgood to me." Probably, Erica thought, because she had forgotten her married name. "What wonderful memories I have of my little girls. They can't take those away from me. What glorious days on the *Exile II*. I can see you as clearly as if it were yesterday, diving off her side . . . you can't swim in the bay any more. How you could have forgotten your Aunt Trudy all these . . . how easy it is for the young . . . Erica, Erica, you were always a little fraidy-cat and Billie, Billie was as fool-hardy as my beloved Tom. Do you remember how crazy you were about tomatoes? What little devils you were . . ."

Erica smiled away but to herself defended her past. There was one devil and one only average. And also she had never been crazy about tomatoes, the color of which Aunt Trudy was now as red as. Hypertension, Billie had said. Erica turned the talk to peaceful Honora and soothing Lucy and the Ives grandchildren, who, as it unhappily turned out, were an explosive subject.

". . . hasn't spoken one word to him in nearly two weeks. Total silence. It's not right. After all, Tim's not yet twelve. But I blame Billie. I blame her although she is my own daughter. She ought to know Sam by this time. If Sam's certain Tim's lost the rudder and is lying, then Tim ought to admit it and apologize. That's all. Well, Billie won't make him do it. She says if he didn't lose the rudder why should he apologize? What kind of a lesson in honesty would that be? What I say is how about a lesson in respect for their father? That's what I'd like to know! The fact is, Erica, and I can say this to you but I can't say it to anybody else, those children have never been taught to . . . Billie's made a very slack . . . I am their grandmother and nobody loves them more than I do but . . ."

Erica was touched by how commonplace a figure this mighty woman cut now. Out of everything in Moriches, the bay, the creek, the houses, the only thing that had in reality lost dimension was Aunt Trudy. A little red chiffon was tied around her pale frowsy head. Her face was pouched and damp and powdered and damp again. Her lipstick was lipstick red.

". . . really it is quite a comfortable estate. They call it 'Hitherto'—interesting? Well, Sam was going to be a writer when he was young. A poet manqué, poor fellow. Medicine's gain, I suppose. There are different temperaments, Erica. You have to make allowance for different temperaments"— and she lowered her lids against those who had not made allowance for hers—"but she won't listen to me. One of these days some little nurse up at his hospital. . . . I may have my blind spots but I know men. I understand them. They're like children. You have to make them believe they are the center of the universe. Otherwise they become very restless. They can't help it. It's not in their nature to sit by the hearth . . . roaming is their instinct . . . they're tom cats. My poor Tom . . . it's all biological. A man wants many women but a woman wants only one man. It's the essence of the tragic condition . . ."

Billie rescued Erica.

Chapter 15

For the rescue Billie wore tight white jeans and a dark blue shirt of a silkish jersey, very careless with nearly all the buttons undone, and no shoes. Her brown feet matched her brown face. You could see a lot of her handsome bony breastbone. Erica was in just an orange dress.

"What are you-all talking about?" Billie asked in a grinning greeting. She had a slight southern cast to her speech, owing probably to living on the south shore of Long Island. Anyhow, she said you-all sometimes. Her mother, who was not often actually asked to say something, repeated her summing-up statement on the male-female situation in an important voice: "It's the tragic flaw and it's the human comedy. I've always maintained: biologically speaking, a man wants many women but a woman wants only one man!"

"It doesn't speak well for Darwin, does it?" Erica said, smiling into Billie's grim expression. "I mean, one would have expected a better sort of adaptation, more promising for the survival of . . ."

"My opinion is exactly the opposite," Billie said firmly. She was certainly going to prove a hard-hearted daughter. "First of all, we are not surviving, and second of all, the men I know are yearning to be monogamous but the women I know . . . aren't. It doesn't even matter whether they are nice or not."

Since neither the mother nor the daughter had the expectation of being enlightened by the other's philosophy they didn't listen to each other and Aunt Trudy asked as if it followed, "Has Tim given in? You can speak openly. Erica knows everything."

"Goddamit, Mother, why do we have to wash our dirty linen in front of Erica?"

"Erica? Erica is family," she said complacently. Erica smiled foolishly.

"Does she understand, Mother, that you absolutely worship Sam so that you are more than happy to spill the entrails of all six of his children on his altar, to say nothing of his wife's?"

"I've got to go home and wash my own dirty linen," said Erica. It was going to be too much for her meticulous nature, and she got up.

"If somebody doesn't look after that man he'll just walk out!" the mother warned the daughter. "You're not in your first bloom of youth, you know. You live in a fool's paradise, Billie. He's terribly attractive. You've seen him, Erica. Would any woman turn him down?"

"Never!" she said, and did not repress a laugh.

But she left the two women to wind up their session in their own way and walked home. What an awful marriage, she was thinking, and nothing to hold it together, not where children are so grossly used as counters. It could scarcely be for the benefit of the children . . . Sam was pitiful but Billie was indefensible. Why either of them stood it . . . it really would be a wonder if Sam hadn't found comfort in a little nurse . . .

And the morning finished out with Erica having transferred her attention from the bit of gravel in her own marriage to the pending collapse of Billie's, and she transferred her indignation as well. Sam was a bully and a peacock. Erica could not even have sustained an interest in him, pretty as he was, except, as he had put it, for old time's sake. Against Billie, only a half-sister but a full-grown consenting adult who had locked herself in with baby after baby, she delivered a stern judgment, so that by the time Billie turned up Erica had gotten the whole wretched picture of Billie's life quite clear and was able to take the liberty of asking in sorrow and in anger why she kept up the farce of such a marriage—it was clearly no profit to the children, nor to Sam—how could she live out her whole life a charade? But Billie, taking her completely by surprise, said it *was* a profit to her.

"It's efficient," she said. "It may throw those looking at my life from the outside but from the inside none of the possible alternatives would be an improvement on what I have now. There isn't a day goes by that I don't look them over just in case I miscalculated. I live by the Principle of Efficiency, if you know anything about economics," she grandly. And so Erica thought it was money.

But as Erica confidently misassumed a life of misery for Billie, she was the more fascinated, as the story rolled out, to be entirely disabused. Billie was the very farthest from being miserable. It is true she took a hard look at each new day but it was still the pleasures therein she found sufficient. There were three elemental needs, Billie said, she had to satisfy and none of them was money, and she had never been able to see any other arrangement that would be better than what she had. The children's welfare was the first. If she left Sam she would have to rear them all by herself and she couldn't stand the bookwork—the simple clerical complications of living without a man—and the last thing she wanted was to be married to somebody else because she'd have to take on *his* children. It would be absolutely inevitable at their age that he would have children and she really hadn't the emotional capacity to extend herself to another little creature. It would wash out the summers, her best season. And besides, remarrying would impinge upon her second cardinal need, which was space. She couldn't stand to be closed in and she needed space. People criticized her for the great disorder she lived in, and Sam had a fit about not having meals on time and so many people coming and going, but disorder gave her space. She hid in it. After all, wasn't Erica with her tidy responsible life totally accountable every minute to everybody? Anyone could put his finger on her whenever he pleased. Well, with Billie one could not. And God knows it wasn't a question of her being wicked and immoral in her private time, try as she might. Sex was her third need.

"I suppose you never had an affair?" she asked Erica.

"You mean besides the one little moment with Sam? No. I know it sounds stuffy but it's a consideration that hasn't ever come up. Yours is a much more sophisticated way of life, Billie. Our academic world is different. There've been an awful lot of divorces lately . . . I mean people around us are splitting like amoebas, but I don't hear about actual love affairs until they've left home, as it were. I don't think you can keep an extra woman on our salary scale, actually," she concluded, with a shy smile of apology.

"Oh hell, Erica, everybody thinks the next person has a fantastic thing going. You read these surveys about how high the rate of infidelity is, but I know damn well when they go around with their polls, people just lie. It's their romantic outlet. I don't know anything harder than getting an affair started and I think they're just bragging."

They were now back into the subject about which Erica felt least easy. She was really only comfortable aboveboard. Not old honest Billie, evidently.

"There have been some men," Billie said, ". . . well, actually only three in my long life . . . who really excited me, and I know that I . . . I'm quite sure they found me attractive," explained the all-time knock-out with engaging modesty, and then with a sigh, "Well, you know how these things go. They wonder whether you ever get to town for lunch some time . . . and then there you are driving in every Tuesday to meet at Pavillon. And after a few weeks the tension has built up wonderfully until finally they can't fight it any more. They've fallen madly in love, they can't work, they can't think, they know it's insane but they've got to have you if only you'd just be willing . . . and I say Yes, I *am* willing and I want to." Billie stopped.

"And then?"

"And then that's it."

"What's it?"

Billie took a patient look at the sky, horizon to horizon, and said, "Then they back down."

"Back down?" said the echo.

"You know what it is, Erica. Men—our sort of men, or at any rate *my* sort of men—really don't like being unfaithful. They have a cautious protective decency that's part of what makes them so attractive. . . . If only their wives would stop being neurotic! And perhaps to be absolutely fair they'd better give them one more chance! Or they can't risk exposure because the children are still so young. But what really is the truth is they Just Don't Dare, they just don't dare," she repeated, in a voice that carried some sympathy for them. "I suppose you have a thousand moral qualms?" she asked, and then added, "I haven't one. But do you want to know something? I've never slept with any man but Sam. It would certainly shock a lot of people to know that. Even *you* . . ."

Erica watched and listened with a silly smile of sympathy and thought wasn't this the saddest damn story? Not too sad. Billie had had those three longish-run approaches. And they were terrific times, incredibly stimulating, she knew she never looked better than when she had something going. It gave her good color. What she really had a taste for was the adventure, to be into something clandestine and illicit—she could taste the excitement—and *comic*, it was a comic adventure, you had to laugh at yourselves, and at the same time it was freeing, immensely freeing. Besides being *educational*. "Do you know it's a sociological fact that all love affairs are alike? They begin with a tentative suggestion about lunch— it *has* to be lunch—on Tuesday at Pavillon or the Colony—I don't know why Tuesday—by men whose wives have become very neurotic and drink but they stick it because of the children. And it's all on the government, all tax-deductible . . . pays for the bombing. Except Robbie. The Algonquin, he said. I don't know a man more attractive than Robbie. Do you think so too?"

"Yes," said Erica, undone by the Algonquin.

"I'm dying to meet Frank. Is Frank a lot like him?"

"I don't think they have anything in common but their long legs," Erica said finally after sifting through several comparisons.

"The night of the fire," Billie said, "he was just a race apart. That long easy stride . . . my God, he's a huge man, but very graceful, very light on his feet. There were four people who were hurt badly and they were on the shore and we wanted to bring them to these pallets that we'd fixed in the huts. I think I'll never forget Robbie. He'd pick each one up very gently and carry him in his arms and I followed . . . I'd watch his legs—his trousers were still wet and clung to his thighs . . . you could see the long thigh muscles by the light of the burning boat. He was so limber, so limber. . . . Well, the next year somebody had this terrific idea about the survivors, d'you know? We'd meet at Stresa, you know about that? And I wrote to Robbie and said I'd come if he would, straight out . . . Jesus, I've had a real thing about him . . . I can't make him out . . . he's not like any other man."

"What happened in Stresa?"

"Nothing happened in Stresa. We drove to Milan and Pavia and Sirmione because he wanted to see where Joyce met somebody or other, and we stayed the night afterward in Verona and nothing happened in Milan, Pavia, Sirmione, or Verona, where the hotel was crowded and the desk clerk was quite exasperated with him for wanting two rooms. I asked him once, 'Robbie, do you find me attractive?' and he said very warmly, 'You know I do, Billie.' I just don't think he's gay. Do you think he's gay?"

"No."

"Well," Billie sighed, "I put it down to the early religious warping . . . there's something about the priest in him. Otherwise I can't account for . . ."

"And it was every Tuesday at the Algonquin?" Erica could not forbear to ask.

"No, just once. After all, he lives in Boston."

They came back to the subject of Sam. Billie said there wasn't a single word he said with which she agreed but by keeping the noise level very high she didn't have to listen. Erica's heart had been going up hill and down dale as Billie talked but Billie stayed beloved. Only in regard to Sam was Erica provoked to make a judgment.

"That's terrible, how you shut him out altogether like that," she said somewhat sternly. "A man really ought to be allowed to think himself of some use. I wonder he takes it."

"He knows he's some use. Sexually we're very compatible, we're very well matched in bed. When we don't talk we make a great pair. He knows if I didn't have him every night I couldn't stand it."

"Every night?" Nothing Billie had so far said was so astonishing to Erica.

"Well, not when I'm away," said Billie reasonably, and then added with kind tact, "of course I know I'm very lucky to have Sam."

Erica bridled at the idea of such a marriage and was reduced to silence. It sounded like what happened when you married the gamekeeper. Finally she said pointedly, "Under the circumstances I suppose Sam can't have gotten the little nurse."

"Really, I think our . . . I think it is precluded. Do you wonder whether Frank might have a little . . . lawyer?"

Erica laughed. Billie had small regard for her tendency to moralize and refused to be improved by her. In respect to the substance of the question of whether Frank might have a little lawyer, Erica explained finally and helplessly that he was simply too busy. He was always accountable. And moreover, she told herself but not Billie, when Frank heard this sort of gossip about other people he held them in contempt, speaking confidently for Erica as well. Erica might sound a little stuffy but contempt was too strong to describe her judgment, were she to have spoken for herself.

"What I don't understand, Billie," she said, "is why if things are so fine with Sam *that* way, you would want to find . . ."

"It would just be a damn sight nicer to make love with a man you love, that's all."

And when Billie was about to leave she said to Erica, "Well, you are the only woman I know who claims to be really satisfied with her marriage—and I don't believe you."

Erica laughed again and marveled that Billie might have an exit line for every exit.

Later, before dinner, in the kitchen Ellen said to Erica, "I can't get over what Moriches has done for you already. You're simply blooming."

"Oh, it's probably Billie, Ellen. We're poring over each other obsessively. Just the two of us, we make a regular encounter group. I think I'll never be the same again."

"I have a very small regard for encounter groups," said her mother primly.

Chapter 16

The events of the summer began to follow little wave upon little wave. Also the nonevents. None of the waves brought a note in a bottle from *Whitewood's* magazine. None of them carried Robbie back from Boston. Ellen and Simon Caplan flew off to California to visit Wilson, who was not well, and Erica stopped being anybody's child. Her own children moved nearer to their seasonal dispersal. All the Ryans had met all the Iveses and returned to their respective homes to deliver their opinions. The run up to Westhampton was only twenty minutes, and beforehand Erica was shy of venturing her values among the upper classes but immediately upon being met they reduced themselves to a level a trifle beneath her own. The children of that old Republican money were giving pool parties for the Black Panthers and the peace movement. Erica did not laugh at them a lot. Billie in fact laughed more. In regard to being the object of derision, Billie said, "The intellectual left are too sensitive to mix napalm with Bloody Marys. Well, it's easy for me to write a check.

It's harder to be thought a fool. But in order to get the money they need willing fools. I let them have me. That's what I contribute."

When Frank at last came down to Moriches for a run of days he met Billie and did not like her. But Billie was safe in Erica's private preserve and fended his criticisms. Frank liked Sam, to be contrary. About Billie he said with distaste, "She sleeps around."

"How do you know?"

"By looking at her! Or I should say by how she looks at me. I don't like to see it in a woman."

"What about in a man?"

Frank dismissed the question as if it were not worthy of his attention and Erica didn't press it. She was chary of letting him into her musings about Billie. They would have bored him anyway. He was abstracted by his own thoughts and they put him in great spirit. The marks of attrition from that long awful year ought to have been visible, but they weren't. Something was up his sleeve.

In the privacy of her mind Erica recoiled from Billie's marriage but admired what Billie in justice called its efficiency. It was hard to feel sorry for Sam. He wished to be that sort of cock of the walk and evidently he had something to crow about.

"I would have misgivings if I thought that son of theirs took up with our Lucy," Frank said. "Billie's assigned them a sailing date. I was right there. He looks like a poor starter to me. Billie said she wanted to talk to me about him, that Sam was awfully disappointed he didn't get into Princeton. But, she said, he wouldn't have gone anyhow because he wanted to write. 'What were his Board scores,' I asked her. 'Oh,' she said, 'something like 780 in math but he didn't crack 500 in the English.' And this guy wants to be a writer. Well, it's no concern of mine what the hell he does as long as he stays away from Lucy."

"Oh, I agree entirely," said Erica, who agreed entirely. "Only I think Lucy really cares about her young man from Amherst. She won't just sail off with somebody else."

"Don't you believe it! If there was ever a washout it's Lucy's whatsisname from Amherst."

"Well, we'll see. She'll only be down here another week." Erica was doubtful enough about the relationship between Lucy and whatsisname. They were sweet and loyal to each other, like playmates, and both redheads and both wanting to work with retarded children, and they slept together. This Erica the mother was allowed to understand ostensibly for her wisdom in regard to the contraception problem. It wasn't something the father was to know. It troubled Erica. She found that she did not grieve for the loss of innocence. She grieved for the fact that it wasn't lost, that sex ought to have been harder to approach, more difficult to arrange, more exciting or forbidden, more of a climax, so to speak. But the folkways of freshmen were sunny as fairyland, it was Summerhill everywhere, although, she thought gloomily, more dark disorder brooding underneath than ever.

Between the two Iveses, Erica's own sensuality was flushed out. From inside her skin she felt the physical self-awareness of a high school beauty queen. Her state of mind, if it could be called mind, was not only unprecedented, with the dimly remembered exception of those weeks when she was twenty-one, it was untimely in the extreme. It was untimely because of her age and it was hardly in line with the position of the women's movement. She was not unmindful of these fatuities. But in sexual matters the head does not lead. In the many summer evenings that followed through June and into July it eased matters considerably for Erica to feel beautiful. After all, she had to move from the security of her familiar academic world to Billie's, where talking about what you read wasn't the way of life by a long shot.

Fanning out from the old Ives house was a new deck

standing on stilts in the middle of a sea of marsh grass right under the largest sky money could buy. Moving through his guests on the deck was Sam, looking for Erica, singling her out. Everybody else got a lot of scowl and complaining handed over with his drink, but with Erica Sam's brow cleared and he kept her elbow in the cup of his hand and was her shepherd as often as he was able. She watched his face when he talked to her and was set up from the elbow, but put down by the mind. He used it mainly to count wrongs done, and Billie was the big doer. Mark wanted to write and Moira couldn't read and Tim lied about the rudder and it wasn't interesting. Erica said, on the one hand, "Well, Sam, you may be right about the rudder but the punishment is draconian . . ." but, on the other hand, "It certainly seems reasonable that Mark should be expected to support himself if he wants to write. . . . Goodness, Sam," she said impatiently, "you have some parental rights! I can't see why you don't use your fifty percent . . ."

Sam was enchanted to find Erica again, as if she were proof of the fine life he would have had if they hadn't all spoiled things. He could not get over what a beauty she had become, he said more than once, with a touch of resentment as though they had tricked him here too. Erica was amused, a little insulted, but was charitable with Sam for her own reasons.

Billie said two of the men she had been interested in would be there and to look out for them, and Erika made a point of talking to what she thought were the right two. In particular toward a man by the name of Howard or Fowler who was with the International Monetary Fund she felt a rush of tenderness. Billie's honest lust probably frightened him off. She couldn't say, "Look here, Howard, or look here, Fowler, men like you in their forties and fifties are infinitely more attractive than track stars. The very lines in your face are all asset. They are the marks of self-doubt, they trace the deep failure in a successful man and they dearly touch a woman like Billie, and a woman like me. Don't worry too much about the performance you think Billie will expect."

The Ives deck two Sundays running had lots of Fowlers and Howards, nice men, thoughtful, anxious, a little fragile, well-mannered, well-groomed, and their neurotic wives, nice women in expensive clothes, intelligent, better-read than the men, elementally unhappy with themselves. Billie looked the best. She looked like a woman who must have known some superb moments in her time. It just probably scared the hell out of most men to try and match them.

When they were driving back from the second Sunday party, Frank said, with warm affection, "Well, there are a lot of good-looking women in that crowd but there isn't one I'd trade for you. You're head and shoulders above the lot of them. I mean that, you know."

Goodness, she thought, of all the men to be going home with, the one who finds me wholesome! But she received his compliment in silence, which Frank might have mistaken for modesty. Her jaw jutted into the dark.

"Listen, girl," he said, "I was going to wait until things firmed up a bit more. I have something tremendous to tell you."

Tremendous for him, you can depend upon it, was her thought.

"Hatfield College is looking for a new president and it's more than possible they may offer it to me."

"Hatfield College!" she said in a voice that expressed her astonishment. "Isn't that incredible! Why, how wonderful, Frank! That's what your mystery was all about, wasn't it? Well, they couldn't make a finer choice than you." She was really stunned, taken altogether unaware and her petty self was swept away. She nuzzled her head against his driving arm and told him how proud of him she was, and he took his hand from the wheel for a moment and patted her knee. The thing had gotten started in the early spring, he said, and he'd been up to Hatfield once and tried to look at it through her eyes. They had known Hatfield when they were young because it was in the cluster of colleges in the Connecticut Valley of which Smith and Amherst were part. It shared their excellence and all their problems except the coeducational one, since it was founded in 1832 on the bicentennial birthyear of John Locke for the instruction of qualified young women as well as men.

The implications of a change like that were immense, and Frank talked to Erica for hours into the night on the screened porch. Finally he said, and as sincerely as was reasonable for an ambitious man, that the only consideration he might give to turning the offer down concerned his quitting on his own people. It was unquestionably their time of crisis, he said, but then it was everybody's. He'd been there sixteen years and you could read it two ways: he was deserting them for private gain, or it would be to their benefit to be free of such an entrenched dominating personality as his.

"I'm suddenly prepared to give a lot of weight to the idea that what they need is a fresh approach," Frank said with a laugh at himself. "What do you think, Erica?"

What did Erica think? Would Frank really have wanted to hear it? The first wave of her admirable selflessness had long since subsided as she listened in vain for some recognition that she would have to sacrifice her own plans for his. Her interest in being a president's wife, or in the reflecting glory, had dwindled quickly. Frank had noted for her sake that their house would have Palladian windows and a butler. He said he was sure she could charm it into something as livable as they had now. It hadn't crossed his mind to wonder whether she wanted to leave every soul she loved and everything she cared about to charm a strange house a hundred and fifty miles away. Certainly Frank had not meant to overlook her feelings. Had he known, he would have said something. But he didn't know and she didn't tell him.

It was Frank's innocence that revived Erica's silent determination to defend her own territory. She sat listening to him, smiling through her part, and didn't rise up and shake him and say, "What about me? What about me?" Besides her friends and her old livable house, she did not want to leave the city she adored, whether or not she was the last human being to find New York adorable. But above all she was crushed by the oblivion into which Frank cast her serious effort to individualize herself, or restore her sense of personal worth, or whatever it was that was hanging upon her application to *Whitewood's* magazine. He did not seem to wonder how she was to get back and forth to Madison and 48th Street every day.

"They've heard an awful lot about you," he said. "That's why I think we've got it in our pocket. I expect we'll be summoned up to Hatfield very shortly and as soon as they meet you . . ."

They certainly didn't intend to buy a pig in a poke, did they!—that was what she thought about that invitation.

". . . another fellow from Wisconsin is the only serious consideration but he has the problem of a wife who's a pediatrician or something and doesn't want to leave her . . ."

Erica broke into tears from the confusion of her emotion and it passed for joy and the menopause. Frank comforted her and they went up to bed and he made love to her for the first time in a long time, through which she could not quite stop crying.

Chapter 17

Erica presided over her life with a seeming calm through the whole of July and into the first few days of August. Her original pique with Frank was so fierce as to seem outlandish and caused her to leave things as they were until she could talk to him reasonably. But things would not stay as they were. No sooner had Frank been allowed to believe that the Hatfield job would almost certainly be offered to him than he was warned by a friend on the committee that the selection was once more in doubt. In fact it looked, said the friend, as though the fellow from Wisconsin would be the one, pediatrician or no pediatrician. Frank was deeply disappointed, how deeply only Erica would know, and her heart went out to him and her pique quieted. Nobody else had the least idea this thing was in the wind. Then unexpectedly at the end of July they were both invited to Hatfield for the weekend and the light came back into Frank's eyes. The morning after that portentous and secret visit, Billie, in a temper, kicked through some slats from inside her mother's side of the hedge and came storming through.

"Goddamit, my mother's red as a beet, she drinks like a fish, and she lies like a trooper." She said, "Sam says she's red from the hypertension pills but her liver is enlarged and she'll be dead in two years if she doesn't lay off the bottle. Now how the hell are you going to make her give up her gin when she denies ever touching it? She swooshes her mouth with cologne. Jesus, I've been buying her Arpège by the bucket for years. I couldn't understand how she went through it! I said I thought she must be drinking it. And by God she was!" Billie and Erica were on the top step of the porch but Billie said she was itchy so they went for a walk. It was a hot afternoon. Her mother was not what Billie was itchy about. It took a long time to find that out.

"I don't know what's got into Sam!" she said finally. "I've never seen him like this before. He's furious because Mark wants to take the year off to write. I said, 'Well my God, Sam, you took a year off to write,' but he said *after* he had his degree. After. Mark's got to get achievement-oriented! Well, you know, shit, how you going to get Mark achievement-oriented *these* days? Everybody he knows is stoned, for God's sake. Sam says if he doesn't go to college why should he get an allowance? Now that's just vindictive, I think. And Mark's only nineteen and really"—and here her voice broke with tenderness—"he feels there's a book inside him. I think it's a very bad idea to repress . . . but Sam can be so stubborn. Now he says he's the father, he's entitled to half the voting rights, and with his fifty percent he says Mark should get a job or go to college."

"Well, you have fifty percent, Billie," Erica murmured, meaning to even out her influence. "Is it going to be a draw?"

However, it was more complicated, and in fact it was crazy and actually it was not precisely about Mark . . . actually it was more about *Lysistrata*. Sam, without evidently needing to spell out the terms, had simply been going to bed every night and turning his back to her.

"Oh Billie, I don't know whether to laugh or cry," said Erica, and broke up. They both laughed until they staggered. Then Billie, having the whole lot of unused sexual energy, mounted a counterattack. All right, it was very funny but what would Erica do if she were blackmailed like that? Erica said she wasn't susceptible to it. She wasn't sexually a very excitable person. She said the liberation movement had established that women were entitled to experience every sort of sexual response and she would take the opportunity of admitting a small need and not blush for it.

"You mean not any man? Or just not Frank?" Billie asked as if she were talking about a pear and an apple.

"Oh, Billie! For heaven's sake. I'm not indifferent to an attractive man, but . . . my mind doesn't play with it, that's all."

"I don't think you're being honest," said Billie, not in rebuke, but as though after pinching it well she decided the pear was bruised. Erica, who had so lately been pleased to discover how unhonest she was, and who in fact was still in the flush of pride over her peerless performance of unhonesty before Frank who remained absolutely distroubled by a doubt about her . . . and before the Hatfield trustees, laying out all her most admired attributes, wearing her beige linen dress and not rolling her peas onto her knife . . . Erica knew *of course* she wasn't honest. Only she didn't exactly know she wasn't precisely honest on this point. Billie was stirring up the bottom of her. "I mean, the way you talk about Robbie," Billie went on reasonably, "I just don't believe, frankly, that you aren't in love with him."

"Oh for crying out loud, Billie!" Erica said with impatience—and then blurted, "How can I love my husband's brother?"—and felt tears sting her eyes.

"Oh God, Ric, I'm so sorry. I didn't want to poke into something that painful," Billie said, which wasn't all that honest in *her*. They had come to a little bridge and were leaning over its rail looking at a lovely cove bordered by leafy trees and grass and on one side a long elegantly designed white-painted fence perfectly reflected in the still water. There were two little white boats tied to two little docks. Everything had the appearance of innocence in duplicate.

Erica drew herself up and said sternly, "You're going to make too much of this, Billie. Something has come up that's put me under a strain and I'm sworn to secrecy about it but I'll tell you. We didn't go up to see Honora at camp. We went up to Hatfield College to see whether they want to have Frank be its president." Boom, bang, pow. Billie said it was terrific and incredible and what would Erica do if she got the job at *Whitewood's*?

And because she thoughtfully asked that question Billie got a widely ramified, discursive, long, and tearful answer. She had gnawed and gnawed at the base of Erica like a beaver and finally Erica toppled.

To begin, Erica told her all about being the princess and the pea, but wound up very justly with a warm testimonial to Frank, who was much nicer than she and she couldn't mean anything more.

"It's really true," she blubbered, "it's really true that he is a remarkable as well as attractive man, a fine, gifted, guileless —absolutely guileless *with me*—humble, thoughtful, *over-bearing* man." She was back into her anger. "'It is his definition of me that I am! He defined me from the beginning and then I've just been literally grammatically obedient. Well, I've got to be free of it! It's like a second weaning. I want a room of my own. No, I don't mean really a room of my own, but I want *room* . . . I'll tell you what it is I crave—my own private domain upon which not another living soul has authority above me. Or thinks he has. Or around me! I need a moat. It's a screaming necessity. Ohhhhhh, Robbie! He's watched this coming on!"

"What does Robbie say?" Billie asked.

"They can't stand each other. They can't stand each other because each sees mortal contempt in the other's eyes. They've always split me down the middle, those two. What would it profit me, Billie, to entertain fantasies about Robbie? *I've* spent twenty years bestriding the two of *them!*"

"It would get rid of a lot of your tension," Billie said, not specifying 'it.'

"Oh, for goodness' sake, Billie, anybody else would say take two aspirin. Not you."

"Now that Frank's going back to New York do you think Robbie will turn up? It's been a long time. I haven't seen him to say hello yet. It must be more than a month," said Billie, nudging and coaxing her subject along.

"It is seven weeks, three days, nineteen hours . . . is that what you want to know? But what seems so fascinating to me," Erica said, intending to foil Billie, "is the . . . the evidence of those lurking subconscious forces that build up their own momentum in one, and one is simply unaware . . . one is calmly riding above it simply unaware. I really thought of myself as Madam Pangloss, that I have had the best of all possible lives, and that is true. That continues to be true, but simultaneously . . . in the best dialectical manner . . . I feel a great surge of frustration with it . . . with myself, with Frank . . . I have examined again and again whether the honorable thing to do is take a deep breath and haul Frank way down to hear my petty grievances. He would certainly think they were petty. Well, he would not know what the hell I was talking about . . . he hates anybody's being trivial. The first meaning of his definition of me is that I'm not trivial . . . and meanwhile at this moment he's rising to such a commanding height. I would not in conscience bring him down if I could."

Erica was herself standing very low, on the little bridge, her back against the rail, talking into the touching country beauty of Moriches, which was flat, but where the trees were green, the sun was yellow, the sky and the water companionable blues.

"Do you think Robbie is in love with you?" asked the indefatigable Billie.

"In love with me, Billie! In love with me! It's indefensible, don't you see that? One's brother's wife! That way lies madness. And damn it, where is he? I'm unstrung when he doesn't check in. That's probably what's the matter with me. He's my ballast. I took a pot shot at him when he was down in June. I've never done that before. I don't even remember what it was all about, but next thing he was gone, without a goodbye. . . . It's been one crazy summer . . ."

"Why don't you call him and tell him you're sorry?"

"Well, I thought it would sound presumptuous . . . for me to suggest, you know, that some flippant thing I'd said made all that much difference to him."

"Do you think he's as hung up as you are about this business of loving his brother's wife?"

"Goodness, Billie. It hangs everybody up. Would you sleep with a brother of Sam's?"

"Oh well, they're disqualified on other grounds. One of them is a Man of the Cloth and the other is a pompous ass who voted for Nixon. I couldn't sleep with anybody who voted for Nixon. But otherwise what difference does it matter who it is? Strictly yours. You're not going to tell Frank. You're not going to rub his nose in it. I have the greatest contempt for people who can't manage these things with discretion."

"You know," said Erica, musing, "people admire Frank for his engaging modesty but at the very core of him he has a ferocious sense of his own manhood which is enormously implicating . . . *his* ideas, *his* children, *his* wife. . . . It makes him very vulnerable indeed, Billie . . ."

"So that's the blackmail you are susceptible to," said Billie at her mother's gate, her exit line for that day.

Erica walked down her own driveway and across the lawn, and the first thing Frank said to her when she joined him by the butternut tree was, "When you want Robbie he isn't around."

"I want Robbie?"

"*I* want Robbie. I want him to order ten copies of Mr. Fitch's daughter's novel *Doubtless Innocent* three copies to be on display in the window and I want him to get cracking and where the hell is he?"

"Which one was Mr. Fitch?"

"He was the one who sat next to you at the brunch on Sunday."

"If you get the job you'll have to do something about the food."

"I knew I had some news that would interest you. Do you remember which one was Boulanger? The one that came with the bimbo? Well the bimbo *writes,* so I said *you* wrote, and that's how we got on to the subject. He's the sort of financier that claims to know that the multidiversified conglomerate holding *Whitewood's* magazine is about to drop it, and it will therefore fold before Christmas. I asked him was he sure because you often wrote for it and would be interested, and he said he was sure and he knew who you were, which was why he was passing on the information."

"That was Sunday, Frank. It is now Tuesday afternoon!"

"Well, I forgot. You'll have to forgive me. I can only say in extenuation that there have been a lot of things on my mind at once, and due to limitation of space I forgot!"

"Did you try to get Robbie on the phone?" Erica asked evenly.

"I tried but he wasn't minding his store. So I was forced to fall back upon my mother, who complained he hadn't been to see her since Friday night. Jesus, what ingratitude! I don't see how he can stand it. He's the only one of her fifty sons and daughters who wouldn't happily pitch her over the ramparts and she doesn't give him a drachma's worth of credit. All I heard about was Mary-Margaret's morning sickness, and the fungus in Eileen's plastic swimming pool in Short Hills, New Jersey. I wonder you ever married me!"

Forgive and forget was what old Frank could do. Erica smoothed her skirt, got up and walked to the bulkhead and peered down for a crab, the last having been sighted in June of 1965, and returned to their white wicker chairs with all her anger intact, not knowing what to do with it. On Frank's lap was the Report of Open Admissions by the Interim Committee of . . .

"I'm sorry about the *Whitewood's* business," he said. "Everything seems to have superseded it. Okay? I don't like to see you mad. . . . Will you do me a favor and see if you can get hold of Robbie tonight? I'll write down everything. Don't be angry . . ."

And when they walked back to the house so that he could pack, he had his arm around her and he was murmuring things about his pride in her and his hope that he would be seen to take his elevation—*if* it was to be—with his terrible boyish glee not showing. They were confident murmurs to a wife who was very torn, very torn between cleaving—and wrenching free.

❁
Chapter 18

Erica wavered uncertainly along the line between cleaving and wrenching free and Frank gave her a pat on the back and pushed her over.

"Well, one thing will have come out of all this, Hatfield or not. You'll have a husband who's a Millennarian. We can have lunch there every Tuesday for a consolation prize," and he went off to New York and his dinner with the trustees at the Millennium, where they didn't allow the wives except on Tuesdays. There were the men who were *somebody,* and there the *consorts,* and how demeaning to be a consort and my God that wasn't where Billie ate lunch on Tuesdays! Billie said she was forty-three and she was only going through once and she was in charge of her own life and she was going to stay in charge. Well, Erica had handed over her charge twenty years ago and now she wanted it back. And how was it possible?

There was a storm coming up but it was nothing to the storm inside her. She cut out across the lawn to batten down the wicker chairs. A dramatic sky was piling up on top of her and she answered the sign with an exhilarating shiver. Back inside the dark house she turned on some lights, checked the windows, and then darted out again through the new hole in the fence to see if Aunt Trudy was properly bombed against her fear of thunder. Nobody answered. Billie must have carted her off. So Erica was out on their stumpy little peninsula alone and she had another shiver of exhilaration for it. It began to rain and in a few drops it was sweeping through the last light of evening, bashing everything on earth. From the window Erica watched the tops of the raging trees against the disappearing sky. At 8:43 the electricity went off.

So that it was 8:43 a long time later when the sky had a million stars and was midnight blue and Robbie came back. Between the quiet drippings she had heard his car even before it had turned into the driveway, indeed, straining, she had nearly heard it crossing the island from the ferry forty miles way. She took her candle out to the porch and watched the wobble of his flashlight, and when he was in earshot she said, "I phoned half a dozen times and prayed it meant you were on your way. I couldn't have made it if you hadn't come back tonight."

"I thought that ferry was going to join the *Titanic*," he answered quietly through the screen. They met in the kitchen.

"I don't remember what I said that made you stay away so long . . . I never want to hurt you . . . I'm so sorry, Robbie."

He didn't answer. She watched him by the candlelight. He was a mammoth hump pulling things out of a brown paper bag on to the kitchen table with a great shadow pulling things out behind him. Onion bagels, cream cheese, new summer tomatoes, *The Odd Women* by George Gissing, a Genoa salami, and two bottles of chianti. They sat down to eat everything but the book. It was amazing how much it took to stoke Robbie.

"You stayed away too long, Robbie. I'm not the same woman. Billie's raked me up."

"Billie? I thought it would be Sam."

"Sam? Sam's too *limp* for a rake."

Robbie was silent and ate on. Finally he said, "I've slipped into assumptions about you and about me that I'm not entitled to at all. You'd never mentioned knowing Sam . . . of course, there's no reason why you . . . it threw me a bit. It certainly explained the mystery of your keeping out of Billie's way all these years. . . . So I thought to myself, if you are going to be in love with him I'm not going to watch."

"You haven't got it straight," she said. "It's a piddling mystery. You're going to be disappointed to hear it." She told him about that ancient romance and he was not disappointed. By candlelight, bending a little across the table, they looked very shadowy and conspiratorial like the conjurors of de la Tour. Robbie asked, What about Billie?

"Oh well, Billie's terrible. And she's full of terrible aphorisms. If you call her on anything she says for goodness sake she's not talking about Middle America."

"For example?"

"For example, men are fundamentally monogamous and dislike having to chase around. Their wives drive them to it. Women on the other hand are inconsolable in marriage. You can't cheer them up. This is because they are by nature *not* monogamous and only a rare few find the institution congenial and they are in Middle America."

"And what did you say?"

"I said my marriage was excellent and she was out of her mind." Erica paused returning Robbie's straight look. "And now it's going to become a little complicated," she continued. "Billie said she didn't believe me. She thought I was in love with you . . . that she herself found you enormously attractive . . . and that your insisting upon separate rooms in Verona would be inexplicable unless, in accordance with the above theory, you are single-mindedly absorbed in somebody else . . . and it must be me. She doesn't mind ceding to me . . . and I . . . I let her cede to me."

Robbie looked so wise and thoughtful they might be talking about the end of the world instead of the beginning.

"I probably do fit Billie's theory of monogamy," he said after testing it in his head for a minute. "But as you say, it's a little complicated. It's true that I cannot seem to displace you. I don't think I ever really try."

He smiled a crooked smile at himself, at Erica, and talked about the complications. He thought he was not ill-designed for the priesthood insofar as he enjoyed the refuge of a single life. Celibacy had not been a painful problem overall, but then he hadn't been celibate. However, he hadn't the acute physical need for women by which other men reassured themselves of their manhood. He thought of himself as a variable on the mild side of this mania and the luckier for it. There were two women in particular he had cared about, and Erica had met them both, but when it came to marriage he thought it would be better to pass his life in gentle regret about not having Erica than in a more lively regret at losing his solitude.

"For the most part," he said, "I've been pleased with the almost nineteenth-century literary style of my life—being the laconic, self-denying, *better* man in an Ibsen triangle . . . not minding self-denial very much. But there have been some black times . . . this last month . . ." He stopped, his chin in his hand, his hair screening his eyes, and forgot to go on.

"What about this last month?"

"Oh well, it was blacker than I thought I wanted to take. There are two sides to the truth and the underside . . . after all, how lonely and pointless and *static* my life seems to have been . . . and when I thought you were diddling with

that silly-ass Ives, well, the romantic fiction of my renuncia-
tion turned to farce—an awful travesty. I really am a character out of Ibsen, one of those in the end too weak to die
with vine leaves in his hair." A sigh went through his whole
hulking frame, and he said, "It's all so unrecoverable, and
was there in that whole past of ours a fork where one might
have taken an alternate path? Any of the three of us?"

Erica had been poking too carelessly at the soft wax by the
candlewick "Oh hell, I've burned my finger! Ouch! Oh
damn it! I can't stand your talking about it's being unrecoverable!" She began to cry from frustration and pain and got up
and rummaged in the dark through the string drawer for
ointment, and said, "If your life has been static, if you've
been pinned in your corner of the triangle, it's as much my
doing as yours. It's been my sanctimony, my preciousness!"

"Now, now," he said, following her into the shadow, putting his arms around her to comfort her for a moment, and
then quickly finding the ointment. They came back into the
light and she put her finger up for him to make it better.

"You ought to hear Billie! She's really a cold bath," Erica
said. "You know, in one way she and Frank are a lot alike.
They're both *un*conflicted. They may be at opposite ends of
the spectrum—she always knows what she wants and Frank
always has what he wants. Oh, Frank is certainly con-
temptuous of those untidy people who are flopping about in
their inner chaos! He has no patience for them. They ought
to pull themselves together. Bombs are dropping, people are
starving . . ." She came to a little crescendo and then de-
scended: "And he's right, I know. He's very fine, Robbie.
I've always hated your hating him . . ."

"I don't hate him. Good grief, I'm very grateful to him.
After all, he's taken good care of you . . . and I love you so,
I . . ." After twenty years Robbie mentioned this, and
went on. "I don't hate him. To my taste his mind's a little
more political, less philosophical . . . in fact, it's somewhat

boring . . . to *me*, of course. But I think he'll make a splendid college president."

"Good heavens, Robbie," she said. "That's a state secret.
How do you know about that?"

"Why, that's right, yes. Well, fellow by the name of
Boulanger's an old friend of mine. He's on the Board of
Trustees up there—at Hatfield. And some time last spring
he talked to me about being on their search committee and I
told him they ought to look into Frank. After all, Frank's
been handling an explosive campus situation very subtly,
very well. . . . They'll be wise to take him. You're not to
tell him that I'm mixed into this, Erica."

"No," she said with a smaller sigh through a smaller self,
and was in her turn thoughtful. "No, it wouldn't be fair to tell
him that, and a lot more." She got up, walked around into
the shadow, and leaned her body against the broad solid
back of Robbie while he sat. She brushed her face in his hair,
which was getting thin, and murmured into the top of his
head.

"Robbie, here's a hypothetical question. . . . If you were
to make love to me you wouldn't draw part of your pleasure
from having a triumph over your brother . . . would you?"

"You know I wouldn't, Erica," he said warmly, and he
reached her round to him while he sat, and with his arms
holding her and his forehead against her breast he said,
"but . . . it *is* a hypothetical question because I don't know
whether or not I can. It's been a long time . . ."

Overwhelmed by her love for him, Erica collected all the
head and chest of him she could and rocked him in her arms
and said, "Oh Robbie, it doesn't matter either way. I don't
love you one iota less if you can't do that. Sex was never love
for me. Just holding you, just being held. . . . This is our
private story, our private truth with nobody measuring, nobody counting . . ."

And it was then that the electricity went on, having the effect of course of throwing a mean clinical light on this odd love scene of theirs. And was there a precedent for such an unlustful illicit affair, she wondered? They came apart and laughed self-consciously and it was like coming out of the movies— Did you like it? Did you think it was realistic? (No.) Do you think in real life one man could eat a foot of Italian salami? Did you notice that the clock had stood still at 8:43? Robbie reset the clock to 1:16.

It might be a mean light but Erica's eyes in a few determined blinks saw where she was and was the more intent upon going on. She had a thrill at having come so far toward breaking from her past or breaking her mold, breaking something, and meanwhile it was not so difficult to be rushing toward the one man in the world she loved with a whole heart. This one man was quiet, turned off lights, put dishes into the sink, was not rushing anywhere. When the two of them were looking at the starlight on the water from the porch, Erica said, "I always adored my grandfather, you know, but once when I came home from college we had a kind of interview and I remember sitting with him, listening, in such a painful state of love for him that I knew I would never know a love like that again. It was my lot, I thought, to pretend to that totality . . . that romantic totality one finds in fiction, pretend to it whenever in the course of time I would have to marry. This was such a fact of life for me, so *integral* to my sense of reality that I never even dreamed about it being otherwise. . . . Then on my own wedding day . . .

"You wonder, Robbie, whether there was ever a moment when one of us might have made another choice. . . . Well, perhaps I could have, or ought to have, at the very beginning. I looked at you when you first came through our door that morning and I think I saw everything . . . well, my God, that was too much—*everything*. I had been going to change into my wedding dress but Simon said we had time for coffee

—do you remember?—and he put brandy in it, good old Simon. I must have shown how near to panic I was. And you looked surprised, Robbie, as though you hadn't expected to like me."

"I was surprised. I'd always been a little annoyed by the achievements of that go-getting brother of mine. I was never sure of what I wanted, never certain I could get it. When I saw you I found it unbearable that he . . . I had a lot of ungenerous feeling to repress."

"And the anomaly is that it's worked out very well for Frank and me. We've had a very good life. And there was even a time when we were still young that he might really have evoked . . . that sort of total . . . totally *yielded* love from me—if *he* had needed to . . .

"Do you know, Robbie, he never looks at me. He wants me right by him, but not so as to obstruct his view. I mean, I know I am his most cherished possession and he keeps me pressed against him but . . . my God, I've lived my whole adult life beneath his chin with my nose in his chest! And over my head he watches to make the next move in his game with life. His romance is out there . . . but mine . . . is something inner, something really where the heart is."

Robbie didn't say anything but took her in his arms silently, uncertainly, wanting to comfort her, and the comforting changed to a charging of sensual excitement in her, and in him, and he whispered, "I think it will be all right. Let's go upstairs."

And upstairs in Robbie's room with the lamp on they went into this with their eyes open, finally reaching what they had been drawn toward for the better part of their adult lives. It was hardly a passion where you ripped your clothes off and got knocked around. It was more of a courtly love, Robbie the aging courtier, touching her and showing her his pleasure, looking after her, not abandoning himself to himself until the end. She was humbled by the sight of his great-sized body with its marks of age, with its unbelievable male organ. For the first time in her life she was an unashamed lover, unabashed by her own nakedness, unfurtive. When she was young the speed and coarseness of lust dulled a lot of the delicate pleasure she took now. When she was young it was a contest, a blood sport, and there were points and you got scores, and a gold medal for simultaneous orgasms which she never won. Well, all of that testing had simply rippled off. Now nothing was close to simultaneous and nothing seemed like failure at all.

They slept and woke.

"Like spoons in a silverchest. I read that somewhere," she said to Robbie.

"That's an old one," he said. "My father used to say that was what marriage was all about when he was feeling sentimental about his. We regarded him skeptically."

They slept and woke and slept again.

"Hey! Somebody's downstairs," he whispered, brushing the hair from her forehead, kissing her awake.

Downstairs Billie at the porch door marveled that Erica could still be asleep. It was nearly ten. Was that Robbie's car in the driveway with the Massachusetts plate? And Erica let Billie in and said Robbie was still in bed and that they'd talked to nearly dawn, and would she put the coffee on while Erica ran up to dress?

"Hell," said Billie. "The two of you alone all night out here . . . I bet it didn't even cross your mind, Erica . . ."

"Oh yes, it crossed my mind, Billie, you'll be relieved to hear. I'll be down in a minute."

Chapter 19

Meticulous Erica was entirely accustomed to having every-thing aboveboard. Anybody might pass a white cloth over the events of her life. Having been this person of spotless integrity for forty-three years, there was the difficulty of an abrupt change. Now showered, dressed, and downstairs again in ten minutes, entirely transfused from the marrow out, she presented herself to Billie believing it was impossible for transitional blotches not to give her away. Billie didn't notice anything. She was riding her own horse.

". . . that anybody would still be in bed, but I had to get out of the house. Sam's kicked up a tremendous row. I hate Thursdays when he's off. And now my mother's there. The two of them . . . I swear, if I hear another reference to his fifty percent . . ."

Erica was listening for Robbie's foot on the stair and hardly heard Billie. Off the top of her head she asked, "Is it about Mark again?"

"No. Jesus. Now it's Christy!"

Billie described the new crisis while Erica kept her back to her by frying a pound of bacon three strips at a time. Her head was spinning but not over the plight of Billie's children.

The true moralist is profoundly bewildered by the experience of intense pleasure even when the cause of it is innocent. Erica might not have been a true princess but she was a true moralist. Her grandfather's granddaughter, it was in the blood. The *coincidence* of making love to a person one loved was almost more than she could manage to encompass, and it left her judgment suspended. She did not immediately regard her act with appropriate cynicism or derision. She was very far from wishing it undone. Instead, and with some degree of righteousness, she turned her irony to the defense of it. Her illicit act had made her an honest woman. Had she never been honest at the core? Well, now she was honest at the core. She had made a clean break with the past, albeit in a manner hoary with age, and now this morning-after she was prepared to believe she'd begun the next twenty years of her life willy-nilly. But if it was a fresh chapter, Erica was hovering uncertainly between two choices just as she had been in the last chapter: whether the new truth would displace the old, or whether the old would make room for the new. She heard Robbie's footsteps.

And there was the magnificent sight of him, with a lot of squealing from Billie, and a lot of hugging, while Erica was satisfied the way one is when the disparate people one cares about are willing to love each other. Robbie lying naked in that bed had looked at one moment like an enormous side of beef. Watching him she had known the artistic pleasure of a cattle dealer. Here he was returned to his own species in tan trousers and a white summer shirt. All the Ryan men wore their clothes well. She found herself sitting down to breakfast at the amazingly same table that had been the chief prop in the shadowy exchanges of the pervious night. Billie, unaware that the earth had turned over, pursued the case of Christy.

Christy was her second son and was entering his last year at Swift Academy. Swift Academy had lately taken in eighty girls, from which Christy had taken in only one. Billie's voice lowered, asking One wasn't a lot, was it? They had been living together through the school year and now Christy had brought her to Westhampton for a visit, and Sam had said, "Separate rooms!"

"It's so goddam hypocritical," Billie complained. "And of course that's the great indictment our children have against us, that we are so damned two-faced. Sam says, 'Fifty-fifty, Billie, and I let you have the better end of the bargain. It's your house, but it's my roof. And I will not tolerate what I consider to be *unseemly* behavior under my roof!' Can you hear him? Can you just hear him? What a hypocrite! That's what happens when you give peasants the franchise. He's known all along about Lisa."

"I don't thing it's a question of hypocrites, Billie," Robbie said. "Christy and his girl don't have to thrust their private relationship under Sam's nose and force *his* complicity. Sam is entitled to his principles as pater familias. He supports the boy."

"He's the first to point that out," Billie said, and sided with the young in their contempt for materialism. Once one got on to materialism everybody could deplore away.

Soon but not soon enough Billie said she had to go. "It's easy for you to *seem* seemly because you *are* seemly," was her parting shot, and she left.

"A bit edgy, our Billie," Robbie mentioned.

"She's in a curious bind," Erica said, and told him that Billie had been sent to Coventry and what her Coventry was like.

"And meanwhile we're in a curious bond." He slipped his arms around her and said, "Let's go back to bed."

"I'd never heard of such . . . well, what must be simply a *physiologic* need. . . . It dumfounded me. Even when I

was young I never . . . but now that I'm old—do you
know an ode to an aging mistress? It's more love than lust
that draws me to you Robbie and that's the truth."

"I know an elegy:

> 'No spring, nor summer beauty hath such grace,
> As I have seen in one autumnal face.
> Young beauties force our love, and that's a rape,
> This doth but counsel, yet you cannot scape.'

Come on, let's go upstairs."

"Donne and I, we're enjoying a revival."

"It ends with something about his not have to go panting
after growing beauties. God knows I'm grateful to you for
that, Ric."

They had until the next afternoon before the music began again and people would resume expecting Erica to
take her place in their lives. Lucy would be coming home
with her father in time for supper.

"Will you leave then, Robbie?"

"Not right away. After all, he summoned me. That's why
I came. All those alarming messages about some book. Erica,
this thing hasn't to do with Frank."

But Erica thought to herself that it certainly had to do
with Frank, that there would be a reckoning. She was not the
same person for him, not decent, not trustworthy. The deed
was done, was incontrovertible, and she assumed that the
consequences must touch them all. She continued to feel
neither guilt nor shame but expected they would be visited
upon her. One morning she would sink with self-disgust. In
all honor, she believed that the thing must be thought
through, but in the spirit of St. Augustine—not yet, not in
these heady hours. There would be time, time for a hundred
indecisions.

The next afternoon several of those had been taken when
Frank and Lucy arrived, Frank superbly happy, confident,

rewarded. "Well, girl, the letter's in the mail. We're home free," he said, and his eyes narrowed and a great Irish grin zipped across his wide cheekbones, down to his pugnacious chin and up again, triangulating his face, and there was Lucy triangulating hers with the same smile but a softer chin. And Erica helplessly and unhesitatingly—but with a sense of *déjà vu*—stepped back to where she belonged. She put her protective arm around her husband, rejoined him, and said she was awfully proud. There was a great hailing of the chief and a toasting, and Frank clapped his brother's shoulder and said, "Robbie, I'm glad you're here. I owe you a lot, old boy. I want to thank you for putting in a word." Murmurs and demurrers. Robbie slipped away, Frank said, "Well, girl, we've probably reached the apex of our lives. Everything's bound to be a little different from now on," and he went up to bathe. Erica slipped off to Lucy's room. Lucy, all coppery from head to toe, looked well but strained when the smile disappeared. The six weeks with the retarded children had moved her very much, she told her mother. She was very proud of those children.

"How's Mitch?" her mother asked.

"He's really fantastic with kids," she said, and Erica heard that as qualified praise. And then Lucy fell into her arms and began to cry with such an awful grief, and it was a hooking of her crook into her mother's heart, making her mother pay attention. Erica flew light-years from her own obsession down to her child's. Mitch was very fine but they had broken up. Lucy thought she could never marry. And what kind of a future could she have? She knew she was a terrible failure but she hated the whole sexual act. And then she could never have children and she wanted children but she couldn't submit, couldn't pretend . . . to love a man . . . carnally. Erica brushed the tears off the freckles and poked her fingers through the short dark red curls of her child, what mothers can do.

"It all starts too soon," the mother said, "and it's all too
. . . unhallowed."

"I just couldn't stand it, Mother, if you said I ought to be
going around with a lot of boys. How grown intelligent people in the name of a higher morality can seriously prescribe
'moderation' with every guy you go out with instead of sleeping with the one you really care about! I think that's disgusting, just disgusting! I mean, intimacy is very private and
you commit yourself entirely . . ."

"Ah, Lucy, commitment, committing entirely—I don't
know that sex should be the seal of that. Women, and I suppose men too, are so liable to be tyrannized by social atti-
tudes, but sexuality is a very individual thing. For some
people it remains obsessive all their lives. But I think it really
doesn't merit all that attention—it certainly can't carry the
weight of one's sense of self-respect or pleasure in life . . .
or a proof of love."

Erica felt a welling maternal need to pass on to her child
as much wisdom—to bear as much honest witness as she
could—to what at least she herself knew. She said that in
her day women were driven into marriage for reasons of
status, and now they were driven into sex for reasons of
status, not a clear gain, she thought. What one needed was a
refuge from being driven any place. She said that Western
civilization, and particularly was it true of their tier of development, was so immensely complicated that the young,
or some young—she herself and perhaps Lucy—needed
more *time*, more time for their complex growth, and that she
thought Lucy was suffering from a too early, too quick, too
total physical involvement but that in time, and through a
more mature love, sexuality would not be such a frightening
achievement test. Gradually you learned the rhythms, the
pleasures, of the person you loved.

"There's too much emphasis now on the right to receive
satisfaction," she said. "A lot of satisfaction is in the giving

. . . when somebody needs you. . . . It's like anything else."

But it wasn't the logic of her argument the mother offered for comfort so much as the historical continuity of her being in her place when her child was in distress. Then her child asked, "Did you feel totally committed to Daddy when you married him, did you love him completely? Or did you have some doubts?"

"Goodness, Lucy, you don't *start* complete. And to commit yourself totally seems to me *smothering*. What one would want to preserve in marriage, I think, is room for . . . well, the discrete integrity of each of the selves. In the finest sort of marriage, husband and wife are catalysts for each other, and Daddy and I are lucky to have the finest sort," she wound up gamely. It was very historically continuous of Erica to say all that.

"Have you ever loved another man?" pursued the indefatigable Lucy.

Erica hesitated and then answered, "Yes, but it's a private matter and I love Daddy and now I'm going to do the wifely thing and cook him a celebration dinner."

Robbie had brought them two bottles of champagne for the celebration dinner, from which Robbie and Lucy, the redheads, glowed alarmingly. So did Erica. Frank, with his pleasure spilling over, even loved his brother, but that night in bed it was Erica whom he loved above all; he told her that, he showed her that. She was in place for him too. And afterward he did an unaccustomed thing by settling himself to sleep against her back.

"My father used to say that a man and wife should sleep like two spoons in a silverchest," he said. "Did I ever tell you that?"

"No, you never did," she said, her eyes staring wide open through the window into the starry night. The wonder was the sky had not fallen down.

She lay still, aware of the stolidity of her own body more than the pressure of Frank's. With all the diverse liens upon her—Robbie's, Frank's, Lucy's, and Billie's—she was incredulous to feel for the first time that she was in charge of her own self, tough and all grown up. No doubt it would pass. The old Erica had been an uncompromising woman. The new had now finished up a spectacular day in which the calls upon her body and soul were so conflicting she would have thought her compliance morally impossible. But just as with the last twenty years, so with the first hours of the next twenty there had been no point at which another choice could be made, another path taken.

"I can't do it!" she would wail when she was a child, about learning to dive, or to swallow aspirin.

"You'd be surprised what you can do," her grandfather would say confidently.

Chapter 20

Erica was engulfed mind and heart by her completed love for Robbie. The little march of quotidian events, however, was leaving neither time nor space for it: other people were not allowing for it at all. Robbie, the lone one, immediately retreated with a book to the edges of their life at the mother house. It was absolutely usual of him to do this. He found a moment from time to time through that next day to let Erica know he wasn't sorry, and to hear that she wasn't.

"I'm reading *Antony and Cleopatra* again. Did you ever read it?" he asked her.

"When I was at school," she said, charmed by his choosing a love story. "I can't remember it at all."

"Well, by God, I've made a magnificent discovery. Do you know how old Antony was in his prime? Fifty-three! My age exactly."

"Fifty-three! How old was Cleopatra?"

"Thirty-nine!"

"My goodness, that's quite heart-warming news, isn't it? Cheer up a lot of people I know to hear about it."

" 'Age cannot wither her nor custom stale her infinite variety'—took the words right out of my mouth!"

And on the next morning the Hatfield letter had come. Swinging through from the post office, Frank set it on the porch table for them all to admire. They all did. They agreed, furthermore, that it called for a great party, a clambake, and settled on the fifteenth when everybody would be home again.

"The fifteenth of August, the Day of Assumption. Very fitting," said Robbie.

"Very fitting indeed," said Erica.

A *Whitewood's* letter was in the same mail, a long flattering *temporary* rejection based upon the present no-hiring policy. Erica flipped her letter on top of the Hatfield one.

"Look at it this way, Ric," said Frank. "The thing's worked out for the best for you. You'd have had to turn them down after all that pursuing."

A sense of outrage flicked through her and subsided as quickly. "Turn them down?" she might have said. "And if I had had *Whitewood's* job when this Hatfield business came up, you would have had to turn *it* down? Which would have been for the best?" Instead she said evenly, "The Day of the Assumption is perfect. I'll call Billie and tell her."

"Fine," said Robbie. "I'll just have time to get a little work done and be back."

"You off? When are you going?" Frank asked. He scanned all data for their utility. "Maybe I'll ride up with you and see Ma."

Immediately an idea came to Frank he was determined to get it moving, and in two minutes he had his hesitating brother finish up his coffee to be on the road. He made one terrific administrator, did Frank. Erica was desolate to have Robbie whisked off so soon.

"I don't like to leave you," Robbie said to her when they had a moment alone. "You're right in the middle of me . . . where there used to be nothing. I hope you'll never regret it."

"It isn't you, Rob. But I've been so . . . *impeccable* all my life. I don't know whether I have the wit to be unimpeccable . . ."

"You're doing admirably," he said with a cheering smile.

"I'm really too disabled by love to be able to think the thing out yet."

"Leave it alone. It's not thinkoutable."

"We've got to think this thing out," said Frank to Erica in their room not two minutes later, freezing her heart.

"What thing?"

"Moriches. This house. It's a seller's market, but fellow I met at the Millennium told me that if we hold on to it, next year will be even better."

"I can't understand you, Frank! Why would we sell this house?"

"Well my God, girl, surely you can see that from Hatfield it's the most inconveniently located . . . you won't be able to get down here for more than a couple of weeks at a time. We'll look for something on the Cape. Jesus, at least we can swim on the Cape."

Frank at his best was a very warm bestower of kindness and at his worst a very cool dispenser of other people's points of view. He had not often dismissed Erica's point of view for the good reason that she had rarely offered a separate one. She was about to now. She was really angry and really hurt by his superiority to Moriches, his insensitivity to the *Whitewood's* business, and was scraffling through her mind for the words to defend the integrity of her own private soul when she caught herself in midthought. She'd done that! Defended her private soul. Integrity was a curious word for it, but that's what she'd done. And wonderfully mollified, she said in a gentle voice and without a trace of chagrin, "I don't want to think about selling Moriches, Frank."

"Fine," he said. "We'll bide our time then. It may yet prove to be a first-class investment."

She let it go, and off the two brothers went, and although

her mother and Simon flew in that afternoon and Honora came home the next, their combined demands made a small dent upon her attention. She thought of Robbie incessantly through the marketing, the cooking, the planning for the party, through her mother's account of Wilson and Honora's fording rapids and portaging and cooking biscuits in the wilderness of Quebec province in a French camp where things were formidable and *en panne* and didn't *marche plus.* Well, Erica *hausse'd les épaules* and hoped she seemed normally responsive. She was amazed to discover how much one heard without listening. She read slowly through *Antony and Cleopatra.* And she resumed her avoidance of Billie.

On the fourth midday of Erica's second twenty years Sam tied up his Chriscraft at the only post along the Ryans' re tuining wall and Erica, with a sign of impatience, went across the lawn to greet him.

"Sam," she said, "you're going to be caught in the rain!" and kissed him easily on the mouth. He put an arm around her, said he had to see her and how about a drink? It was only a little after one, nothing doing about the sun over the yardarm. Well, there was no sun. They walked back with Sam's gin and tonic to sit under the butternut tree so that he could talk to her privately. The sky was gray and heavy, settling in seriously for its annual northeaster; three days of rain and then sun and Robbie and the party, she was thinking.

"I've decided to ask Billie for a divorce," Sam said in a reasonably important voice.

Erica was startled and then furiously angry. She felt on the instant that she was responsible, that she had been flippant about somebody else's life, *Billie's* life, and she was outraged to see what Sam had done with the liberty she had, by inadvertence, shown him that he had.

"That's insane!" she said in a burst of righteous wrath. Her indignation left her for the moment at a loss for further edifying comment but she stared at Sam with such affront one might have expected he would cower and say, "Oh

well, actually I don't really mean a divorce. That's too strong
a word . . ." But Sam was fired by his own inner fury, not
hers. And his face was so aggrieved that in spite of the flattering light cast by the heavy sky he looked like a well-
tanned basset hound. She had to turn her eyes away.

Moira. It was about Moira. She didn't like Sunnybrook
Farm and was wailing to come home. Billie said she needed
to be toughened, she ought to learn to stick things out.

"Toughened!" Sam bellowed in a voice of animal rage.
"Jesus Christ! She wants to toughen a little innocent eight-
year-old girl! What about those boys? What the hell kind of
a perversion is in a mother who . . ."

"I don't understand you two!" Erica broke in a real hand-
wringing anguish and her voice turned to a mourning sing-
song. "How either of you could fool yourselves into believing somebody else would be easier to live with! It defies
belief! You're absolutely ideally suited!" she scolded. "You're
spoiled, awfully spoiled not to *give* . . . to be so ungenerous
. . . both of you! Ach!"

"I'm sorry, Erica! I've had it up to here with her! I don't
have to take all that shit. Billie isn't the only woman in the
world. I happen to know there are decent, kind, understanding . . ."

Aunt Trudy had hinted to Erica that Sam was finding
consolation—if you could call "I told Billie, 'Watch out!
He's having a love affair with Mitzi Wagonback!' " a hint.

"For heaven's sakes, Sam," Erica cut him short. She was
crying with anger and disgust at the string of his awful ad-
jectives. "Whatever became of your civilized understanding
that one makes *accommodations*? Only little children kick
over the whole castle. And do you think that troop of boys
will be better off without you? And how can you part with
Moira?" Tears were streaming down her cheeks.

Sam was nonplussed. He himself was approaching the ur-
bane subject of divorce with urbanity. He said, "Jesus,

Billie's not going to be half as upset! What's the matter with you? Listen, Erica, everybody gets divorced! You're not being reasonable. We can't stand each other."

"You haven't been able to stand each other for twenty years! What gall, *after* you've bred like rabbits, to talk of splitting!" Erica caught herself up. This was not likely to be a winning argument with Sam.

They were standing arms akimbo bawling at each other under the tree, and it had begun to rain. She heard the plap-plap of the fat drops on the leaves, the sound of seconds from a loud clock, and she cast about for another way to stay him. "Look here, Sam," she said in a quieter, voice, "I want to tell you something that I hope you'll weigh. I admit that this summer when we all met again I couldn't understand how you two could have stuck it out. But Billie . . . and *you*, Sam . . . are extremely complex people, and I began to see how you've built your balances and needs and satisfactions into your lives so that in spite of all the . . . grating aspects . . . it is a household with its own rich history and dimension and meaning . . . it answers in a very elemental way for all of you, for the children . . . as a dependable base, as a retreat . . ."

"Not for me! It's no retreat for me!"

"Well it's just exactly there, Sam, just there that you are certainly entitled to more consideration."

"I'll say I'm entitled to . . ."

"Let me finish, Sam. You know, surely, that Billie and I have become very close again this summer, that we've talked quite intimately about . . . you know, more or less everything. And naturally the question came up about . . . alternative arrangements, but she said flatly, and without qualification, Sam, that she did not want to be married to anyone else."

"She did?" Sam was a little distracted and then mad as hell. "Well, she's certainly never said anything like that to me. I suppose I can be forgiven for coming to precisely the opposite conclusion!"

Impulsively, Erica put her arms around Sam and her cheek against his and pleaded, "Please don't say anything until I talk to Billie. For old time's sake," she added with some difficulty. He gave a weary sigh and an assenting grunt. It was raining mildly now outside their butternut umbrella, and, her business done with him, Erica was ready to have him gone. She was a little sickened by him. He had forced her in too close and she felt soiled. "Don't you think with this weather you'd better be off?" she suggested.

But Sam evidently liked to be in close. It gave him the opportunity for maundering in his awful confessional tone. He put his arm around her waist and they strolled to the boat as if they weren't getting soaking wet, and he said, "I've watched you with Frank, Erica. You look at him with such pride, such ungrudging admiration, it just goes right through me. I can't help thinking, my God, for the freak of chance . . . what would I have become with a woman like you standing behind me . . . with *you*, Erica?"

She thought if she were standing behind him she would have pushed him over the bulkhead and let the piranhas eat him.

"You'd better get going, Sam," she said. "I'll call Billie."

Erica ran through the rain to the porch, and was so wet she had to shake herself off before going in. "Ach!" she said to the turn of events.

And on the phone she said, "Billie, I've got to talk to you."

"I've been trying to talk to *you* for days! Come on over."

"We need a neutral place."

"I'll meet you at Blake's Beach. There's that big awning. Nobody'll be there."

Chapter 21

Blake's Beach was a warren of white-painted bathhouses and a roofed deck with deck chairs. It was swarming and cheery in the sunshine with umbrellas and people striped and flowery, but all fair-weather friends. In the rain it reverted to some primordial time before umbrellas and people. Except for Billie's car there was no sign of human life. Except for the sea grass on the dune there was no sign of life at all. Erica had changed to a dry dress and was wearing a raincoat the color of wet sand. This beach was Billie's turf, not hers, and she was a little hesitant to unlatch the gate and trespass and wind round to the deck. Her mood had sobered altogether.

Billie was sitting on the one dry bench against the windbreak in tan jeans and a beige shetland pullover, long-limbed and bent over, resting her elbows on her knees, looking young and vulnerable. She was still Hermes with her cropped pale head: Hermes a little bowed, a little beaten up, it seemed to Erica. Erica sat down next to her on the bench and bent over her own knees. The two women looked across the flat wet sand to the stormy sea, and talked toward it as if it were a mediating party.

"Sam came to see me this morning, Billie. He's very angry," Erica said in a voice gentle and protective toward Billie.

"So am I," said Billie coldly.

"He said he was going to ask you for a divorce."

"Great laugh. He'd never do it," said Billie, unimpressed.

"You'd be surprised what people can do," Erica said, her grandfather's sentence ready at hand. "It may be that you pushed him . . . beyond what he can take. This business about Moira . . . it seems trivial but he says it's the last straw."

"He's not telling the truth. We're quarreling over an abortion, only he's too family-proud to tell you."

"Whose abortion?"

"Christy's girl."

Erica had a weary breath for the way these people managed to grind themselves down, and said, "Well, I suppose a question like that answers itself. What else is there to do? Does Sam have another idea?"

"He's making the arrangements, but . . . I think if it were his daughter he'd haul her up to the arctic so he could throw her out in a blizzard. It's the boys. He beats up on them terribly, he always has. As if he were jealous of them. His mind is absolutely tight closed to what they have to say, how they look at things . . . their life style."

"You know, I detest that term . . . somehow I detest that term Life Style. It invites one to suspend all judgment. It pretends to be libertarian but . . ."

"There's no better person in the world than you are, Erica," Billie cut her short. "And I suppose you're entitled to judge the rest of us sternly. But the rest of us aren't like you. You think we all began at the same starting line and we all ought to be up there with you, superachievers, happy house-wives, model citizens. But you're the only Thoroughbred. You've always been content to stay inside the lines. I never have. When you were a little girl you loved to play house. My God, you still love to play house." Billie stopped to think, and then added, "I'm not good, Erica, and I don't really give a damn." She thought again but she wasn't through: "All right," she continued, "*you're* good. You can't help yourself for that, either. You think the right thoughts, you love your mother and you love your husband and you love your children. . . . Me, I never think the right thoughts and I don't love my mother and I don't love my husband . . . I don't really love anybody but my children . . . and you. Where my children are concerned I'm a tiger . . . and so . . . if it's a choice between . . . if Sam really wants to force me to choose between our marriage and the welfare of our children, I suppose . . . you might say . . . it would be the easiest decision I ever had to make."

The rainy gusts were whipping clear across their deck and both women looked as if they'd been hanging on to the rail of a sinking ship. Billie's anger had made her reckless and she would have been quite satisfied to go down, taking her whole crew with her. Erica was impatient with that kind of recklessness and said pointedly. "You're all wet, Billie."

Billie chewed the wing of her great big sun glasses and considered her misty sister. "You think," she said, "that if everybody pulled themselves together and tried harder their lives could be as peachy as yours. You can be awfully simplistic."

"Well, I'm not so simplistic as to believe *you* are facing an either-or proposition. If it really is the children you care most about it would be a damn sight better to give them *more* father than less. I mean, it's simply naïve if you think you're being noble, saving the children at the sacrifice of your unusual . . . sexual compatibility . . ."

"Oh, sex! That's what I mean about you, Erica. Everything's synchronized in your life. The man you want to sleep with is the man you're married to. For everybody else that would be an astonishing coincidence!"

An astonishing coincidence? Erica heard the echo of an echo, the coincidence of the coincidence. Billie heard her estimate of Erica's naïveté confirmed. She seemed to need to shake it up a little, and said, "I've never thought for a split second that sex makes or breaks a marriage. You can always get sex someplace else. Sam may think he can bring me to heel this way . . . well, hell, I may not be the chairman of the ladies' medical auxiliary but I'm not depraved! My sense of maternal responsibility is really not all that easily toppled! I could even get me to a nunnery. If I thought it was reasonable, if I thought it would be to the children's benefit, I could get me to a nunnery, shit. One thing has nothing to do with the other. I'm talking about a much more elemental sort of decency than sex. I'm talking about the integrity of each one of those children, preserving that integrity from a father who's a goddam bully!"

The gusts of rain couldn't drive them off so a squall was sent across the deck to do it. They had to make a run for it and ducked into the wide commissary doorway, which was deep enough to remain dry. There they propped themselves, each dripping in her own corner, and Erica said with some reluctance, "It's indefensible the way you undercut Sam, Billie."

"What about the way he cuts down the boys? You've seen him. I really would have thought, Erica, it would have gone against your sense of justice. I don't say Christy's been wise about this girl. But it's done." Billie's hard voice softened predictably. "I know he understands how *careless* it was for them not to . . . but they're so young. Do they have to be ridden by guilt for the rest of their lives? Sam's booming imprecations like a Hebrew prophet. My God, everybody's sleeping with somebody else. All the kids are. They feel they're openly, honestly expressing their love . . ."

"Billie!" Erica growled from her corner. "You'll make me throw up! It's terrible what happens to your mind when you turn it on your children. How you can be so unsentimental about the pretensions of everybody else and collapse in a state of maudlin worship before the pretensions of the young! What happens to your critical faculties? Do you really think those boys should be sleeping around in high school? Do you really think that human intimacy should be so casual, that the complexity of intellectual and emotional growth doesn't need as much privacy, as much *time* as society, as the family at least, can provide for it?"

"You're just hung up on sex, Erica. What would you do if Lucy came home pregnant?"

"Oh my God, I'd weep and wail like Hecuba on the walls of Troy and get a good doctor. But I'd certainly want her to know the dimensions of her irresponsibility. I don't want our girls to lose their reverence for life. I don't want them to think abortion is just a medical problem or a legal one. And I'm not hung up on sex!"

"Listen," said Billie in a placatory voice, "I *am* angry about the abortion. I feel the way you do about it. Don't misunderstand me there."

"Oh, I know you do, Billie," said Erica, obediently placated. But having a toe hold on Billie's conscience, she was moved to draw a larger lesson. "You're very odd with your anger," she said. "When a child puts you in a fury you don't turn it back at him, you let go at Sam. Do you see that? It's almost a reflex. Not at Christy for his shocking irresponsibility, not at Mark for his dropping out of school, not at Tim for being careless with the boat, never mind about the rudder—always Sam. You fail your children on two counts, Billie: you don't confront them with your rightful anger, and you . . . diminish their father."

It was a serious indictment one mother had delivered to another for her own good, and certainly unpremeditated. Billie looked out into the rain square-jawed and didn't answer.

"A child needs a strong father," Erica said quietly.

"You can't make a silk purse out of a sow's ear!"

"Yes you can! You laugh at me for playing house, Billie. *Every*body has to play house. In this godforsaken world we all have to play house, women especially. We have to pretend that everything matters—love, loyalty, the sanctity of life, one's family with its history, its duration, its significance, its Thanksgiving dinners and birthday parties. My God, one has to make nine tenths of the whole thing up. *You* have to make up a strong father, *I* have to make up . . ." She trailed off, at an unaccustomed loss for words.

"What do you have to make up?" Billie asked skeptically.

"Oh well, Billie, one can scarcely expect a life without deficiencies," she said evasively. It had stopped raining and she slipped off her sandals and walked to the end of the grey slatted flooring and into the sand. Billie hung back a moment and then joined her and they crossed the wide beach to the water's edge. Billie was still silent, still square-jawed, but Erica was an agitated woman before an agitated sea. She remembered how her grandfather used to say that when a man felt himself losing his will to push on he could find it again at the sea if he knew his Darwin. It would restore his sense of dignity and worth to see what a high place he held next to a mollusk and at the same time give him evidence of his signifying nothing. Erica was finding something of this balance restored in herself. She could once again step back and look at her life with some irony, but Billie's insouciance —or perhaps it was the sight of the sea—revived an elemental need in her to defend marriage and the family specifically for the value of their continuity. She said to Billie that their children only knew a world where everything was breaking up or breaking down. One might at least try to guarantee them their home as an on-going institution.

"Abortion, divorce, they're terrible negations," she said. "I don't mean that I'm against them. You know that. But it seems to me terribly destructive for society if one trivializes them . . . if one doesn't continue to look at them as awesome steps. If a woman's inescapably miserable she's got to get out, of course. But you *aren't*, Billie." Erica's fervor had succeeded in rousing Billie, but, rather perversely, Billie was drawing from this tribute to marriage a great taste for the idea of getting out.

"I'm sure your logic is irrefutable, Erica," she said, "but there's something else that haunts me that I suppose never has haunted you. I don't want . . . when I'm old, I don't want to look back over my life and see just compromises, just adaptation . . . that I never *dared*, you know, to eat a peach . . . I'd like to hear the mermaids singing . . ." She looked out for a mermaid and then went on, "You may be skeptical, but one reason I've stuck things out is because of Sam. I really didn't think he could make it without me . . . bad as he was doing with me. But if he's ready, my God so am I! I'm forty-three. I haven't much more time . . . I just want one good crack at life while I'm at the top of my form. My God, just to spring free!"

"Spring free? It's no way to spring free," Erica said. "Ach! Billie, divorce won't free you from anything. At best you'll have swapped a middling situation for a worse—and especially for the children. I think *really*, Billie, that your instincts have always been right—to accommodate—and that when you look back on your life you won't . . . recoil in disgust at . . . little privileges you've taken for yourself. It's the only way to get through . . . take those privileges and keep your mouth shut and the show going. I've learned that from you. I owe you so much, Billie. I don't want to pay you back with cheap and easy support."

"What are you talking about?"

They had straggled down the beach and now as it was beginning to rain again they were heading back. There wasn't another soul under the heavy gray sky. Everybody was in their houses on the dune playing Monopoly with their children. It began to pour and Erica and Billie had to race, Billie easily beating. They got into Billie's Porsche and she said sternly, "I want to know what you're driving at, Erica."

Erica, short of breath and short of mind, began limply, "Well . . . you talk about different life styles . . . about the children's integrity, and how you are determined to protect it from Sam's . . . intrusion . . ."

"The young today expect to be treated as equals. They refuse to be patronized. Sam . . ."

"I think it's all awfully shallow, Billie. How can I think Lucy is my equal? Why, that would wipe out the twenty more years I've lived. Do I really think I haven't grown, learned anything, become more wise? As the father of those boys Sam ought to be a figure of authority and responsibility, and where you deny him that, you're wrong. His misuse of it, or poor judgment, is, as they say, negotiable. It's not an idyllic marriage but I don't think one of the eight of you wants to see it dissolved. So the crux of it would be . . . whether you could make some decent restoration of Sam's rights as a father, something that would allow him self-respect . . . in exchange for moderation in the exercise of his . . . office. . . . It seems to me . . ."

"Oh God, Erica! You can't change him! You can't change me! I'm sick of it all. I want to get out. I'm sick of fencing and tacking and lying. I just want to be honest. You've been honest your whole life. You don't know what a luxury it is!"

"I'm not honest!" Erica shouted at her indignantly.

"Jesus Christ, Erica, I'm not talking about cutting the PTA. I'm talking about holding it all together. You don't have to hold it all together."

"Oh yes I do!"

Then finally Erica threw her own honor onto the scales, which was like writing her name in her own blood. She told Billie about Robbie and Billie couldn't believe it, she couldn't believe it. And after an appropriate interlude of distraction during which Billie was amused and inquisitive by turns, she fell into a profound silence.

❁

Chapter 22

The rain rained for three days, as did Billie's silence. Erica's anxiety over it displaced her anxiety about herself down to the last drop. She bought steak off the top of her head, bought white wicker chairs until Simon said they had more than Discountland. She brooded and people stayed out of her way, Honora and Lucy watching from the wings until she should be herself again. Ellen, who had begun to write a whodunit, took to her room. Only Simon was busy being kind and handy and thoughtful. Robbie was a lot like Simon. But Robbie and Frank would not be back until the fourteenth, the day the sun was due. And in the meantime Frank called Erica every evening, which was an unprecedented use of the telephone for them. He seemed to need to pore over the smallest details of his thinking about Hatfield with her. (Ought he to drive out there from Boston? Ought he to stay the night? Ought he to rent a car or take Robbie's?) It was not at all like him. At first she could not imagine what point he was trying to make, but then she saw there was no point and was moved.

"What does your mother think about your being a college president?"

"She thought I already was a college president. She wonders why Robbie isn't. Listen, Ric, about this acceptance letter . . ." and it was a detail of no consequence, but how did it sound to her?

On the morning of the fourteenth the sun came out exactly as it should. In the afternoon Frank and Robbie returned exactly as they should, not looking awfully brotherly, and with a large laundry tub of steamers packed in dry ice. Erica was overcome by the dry ice and wheedled her daughters into walking down to the bulkhead to throw it into the creek and watch it and listen about the Schrafft's ice cream and how their mother used to throw dry ice into this very creek, only a little farther up.

The next morning, the day of the Feast of the Assumption, Erica backed her station wagon into Aunt Trudy's driveway to fill it up with her lawn chairs. Aunt Trudy tottered out to greet her in a pale pink peignoir and a dark pink face.

"Isn't it a lovely day for your party, Erica, I'm simply frantic," said Aunt Trudy and gasped and coughed.

"Have you taken your pills this morning?" asked Erica, uncertainly.

"I'm afraid this is a crisis that pills won't help, Erica. I've warned her! I can't fault myself! You're my witness! But she's going to leave him."

"Why do you say that?" Erica asked sharply.

"They have not spoken one word to each other since Tuesday."

"What did she say to you?"

"I know her, Erica, I know her inside out! After all, she's my own child. She adores him—*underneath*."

"Did Sam tell you something?"

"She won't be the first woman to overplay her hand."

"What did she say to Sam?"

"Nothing! Didn't I tell you they haven't said a single thing, either of them, in four days?"

Erica picked up a lawn chair and did not hit her on the head with it.

When she drove back to her own garage Robbie came out to help her unload and at the sight of him her misery spilled over and she played back her exasperating conversation with Aunt Trudy. And then she said, "I always thought when I was little that if you had a real sister you were just ordinary but if you had a half-sister it made you secretly enchanted, it put you into a fairy tale. It was a fateful singling out of the two of you to be one extraordinary whole. Especially Billie and me . . . we're so complementary . . . and this summer . . . it really was uncanny how we came together again, as if there were a magnetic affinity . . . and just at a time when I thought I was slowly suffocating to death, there she was, a fresh wind, a fresh mouth . . . and she lent me her spirit and I came back to life. It's romantic, I know, but I think of it that way. And what have I done in return? Oh God, I couldn't stand it if I were no more than a casual destructive force for her. Do you know what I mean, Robbie?"

Of course Robbie knew what she meant.

"I want her to draw from my strength, go home, and shore up that marriage . . ."

"I think she'll do that," Robbie said quietly.

"Aunt Trudy says she's going to leave him."

"On no evidence whatsoever," he said, hooking a stray strand of hair behind her ear. "She has a nearly spotless record for being wrong, don't forget."

By four that afternoon the Ryans, looking somewhat grim, were all ready to receive their guests. Erica was by now distraught about Billie. But as she was able to be extremely competent and distraught at the same time, all the white wicker was gracefully grouped by the butternut tree, and the long serving table was fluttering with her grandmother's white embroidered cloth. Her husband and his brother the enemy had laid out a wide fire bed of coals and rocks with seaweed they'd brought from Boston. Each was offering a tight-lipped opinion about its improvement which the other did not share. Ellen, the first wife of Tom Thoroughgood was sitting contentedly with Aunt Trudy, the second, who was protesting to Simon that while she didn't drink ordinarily, it was a party and she would have a gin and tonic but without the tonic. Honora and Lucy could only be persuaded into the best of their worst-looking clothes, their thing, but their mother wore a sleeveless white piqué dress, décolleté and flattering, her thing.

One could hear the roar of the Ives' Chris-Craft before it could be made out. Handsome Sam leaped from the gunnels and tied up. Moira was with him, always looking a little teary in the eye, and the two younger boys who certainly did not leap, not "for full jars," not "for fleecy flocks," not for anything.

Sam said, "You look beautiful, Erica, *really*," and Erica asked where was Billie? Sam's face tightened as if he had the lead in the sixth-grade tragedy and he said she and the other children had taken the car.

"I talked to her, Sam," said Erica in an ardent whisper.

"You've wasted your breath. She's as hard as nails. Not like you, Erica. My God, when I think of a marriage like yours . . ."

And there were the rest of the Iveses just coming around the front of the house, dazzling Billie in a white dress too, and the three older boys and the abortionee. Erica gave Billie the pleading look of a sick cow but Billie was hard as nails. Everybody had Frank to turn to and be joyful about, and there was a lot of drinking and an enormous production over the clams. Billie had sidled over to Frank—a good way to avoid Erica—and then later, when they got down to steak and corn, the grownups made an including circle of their chairs while the young went off to sit in a row on the bulk-head. At some point Sam said, "Erica certainly knows how to throw a party."

"Oh, she's in her element," said Frank. "She's a superb hostess. It's her bag." Erica sat looking at her feet.

"Will you continue to write for *Whitewood's* when you're out in the boondocks, Erica?" Sam asked.

"I don't know what I'm going to do, Sam," Erica began, but Frank answered for her.

"Hell, she's going to have an awful lot to do," he said. "There are ninety-one faculty wives, a lot of them of course very young women. And there's a tradition at Hatfield that's really very interesting. President Eastman Harvey, who retired in 1892, after twenty-six years in office, President Harvey was a feminist. He believed the wives of faculty members should be included *comfortably* in the academic community . . . ought to be *peers*. Well, you know, they simply weren't qualified, and so he set up a sort of tutorial under the direction of Mrs. Harvey—who never, to be truthful, sounds as if she had her heart in it, never seems a real feminist. . . . In any case, the wife of the president has traditionally represented . . ."

Erica took up a tray of things and walked out of this very element Frank said was hers. She headed across the lawn toward the house and in a minute Billie was by her side carrying something too.

"Well my God, when you talk about adjunctive faculty wives, you're not kidding!" said Billie. It was the first private word she'd addressed to Erica since their session at Blake's Beach. "He just really doesn't hear what he's saying, does he? Frankly, I don't know how you stand it."

"It's not all that inimical to my nature, Billie, being the wife of a man of consequence, a man with a title. And I've never minded working for my keep."

"Of course, it's terrific," Billie said politely. "But who needs it? Are you really going to be able to endure it?"

"He's innocent, Billie, absolutely innocent. And I've found my way out. I've made it bearable for myself. Of course I'm going to endure it."

"You must need a pretty strong stomach sometimes."

"No stronger than you need. Suppose in the name of honesty I were to say, 'Well, Frank, I'm not straight with you any longer and I've got to clean my conscience.' And tell him the only man I ever loved was his brother. When the smoke cleared, all that would be left would be Frank the sacrificial victim. I don't want him to be a victim. I don't want him to have to pay for this. I'll pay for it myself."

They deposited their respective loads of dishes in the kitchen, where Billie's maid, Anna, was helping, went back out onto the porch, looked to the right where the party was, and turned toward the left and the lilacs. They made their slow and halting way down along the hedge to the water, and across the length of the retaining wall, two women in white looking not in your wildest dreams like a pair of nuns.

"By paying, you mean an uneasy conscience," Billie remarked, after evidently musing on it. "I suppose for a woman with a history of such . . . moral purity, it's not a small price."

"On the other hand, Billie," Erica countered, "I had been feeling increasingly oppressed by a sort of . . . heavy determinism in my life. . . . If I hadn't been able to break through it somehow, would I have continued to be of any use to all these people I care about? The children, Frank, Robbie, my family, my friends, what I think of as my constituency? I might have become some kind of emotional invalid, with the vapors. I don't know. . . . It's true that I may be troubled from time to time by an uneasy conscience, but . . . then . . ." Then Erica turned a beaming smile on her half-sister, and said, "But *then* I will think of your Principle of Efficiency! And *then* will my soul, Billie,

'Like the lark at break of day arising,
From sullen earth sing hymns at heaven's gate!' "

Billie returned Erica's wide grin with a smile of bemusement. They held each other's eyes that extra fraction of a moment in a way that sometimes means there is a new accord. Erica hoped Billie would say a word toward it but Billie did not and they walked slowly back to the party. From a little distance it all made a gracious sight, the boats on the water, the lawn green from the rain, people sitting leisurely in a circle under the tree, their children darting to the edges of a scene Boudin might have chosen for a subject.

Erica and Billie returned to a conversation that was not, however, notably gracious. Mark Ives, the writing son and the one with the most sensibilities, was impressing upon his Uncle Frank, the new president, that the fact of the matter was that he wasn't impressed. He had so far indicted Hatfield for having sold its independence in exchange for government grants (but Frank said they didn't get any) and for ROTC (but Frank said they didn't have one) and above all for its incursion into Cambodia, and now with great contempt said, "I don't want to be rude, but I consider Hatfield among the more insufferably pretentious establishment institutions in the whole fucking country!"

"And I consider you insufferably rude!" bellowed his father.

"Shit, the only son you'd ever be proud of was the one who made a first-class hypocrite!" Mark shot back; but then his mother, who had come up and was standing behind his father, said in a voice deep with anger, "Mark, you are not only insufferably rude to Frank, you show an intolerable want of respect for your father! It's really disgusting to see you sitting there, passing judgment on our lives and values!

If he's done nothing else, your father has spent nearly a quarter of a century treating the sick. Let's see what you'll have done with the next twenty-five years before you size yourself up so grandly!" She then wheeled around and walked rapidly back to the house. She had stunned everybody, left them fixed to their chairs.

Then after a moment Frank got up, took Mark's arm and, leading him off, could be heard to express his hope that Mark would come up to Hatfield to take a closer. . . . And then Sam got up and turned around handily so that Erica could slip a look at his face. His brow was stern but his chin was up. She hoped the not awfully subtle signs meant that he took Billie's rage for an offer of peace.

Everybody resumed being guests at a party and in the best possible taste pretended a scene hadn't been made, Billie and Sam included. When it was time to go, Frank rounded up all the Ives young, very eager that none should be left behind. He sent one division up to the car and the other ahead to the boat. He himself walked between Sam and the sullen Mark, making reconciling noises and patting their shoulders. Mark looked amazingly like his father. Erica gave Sam a wild smile meant for encouragement, caught up with Robbie, and together they went off to say goodbye to Billie. She was in the car.

"I take my hat off to you," Billie said to Erica, then looked at Robbie and back at Erica again. "I *marvel* where your good sense gets you. I wish your good sense were doing as much for me." And she left.